MW01166254

ROAD TO ROMANCE

REBECCA TALLEY

Copyright Notice

DuBon Publishing

Copyright 2022 Rebecca Talley

All rights reserved

This is a work of fiction. All the characters, situations, dialogue, names, and places are fictional and from the author's imagination. They are not to be construed as real and any similarity to persons living or dead is purely coincidental. The opinions and views contained herein are the author's and do not necessarily represent the views of DuBon Publishing.

Except in the case of brief passages contained in critical reviews and/or articles, no part of this book may be reproduced or transmitted in any form, whether that be print, electronic, film, microfilm, or by any other means, without prior written, dated, and signed permission from the author.

Thank you for purchasing this book and respecting the work of this author by not participating in piracy.

DEDICATION

I want to thank the readers who helped me so much with this book. I appreciate your time and attention to details. You helped me make this book so much better.

I also want to thank my readers for their kindness and support. I love interacting with my readers! I hope you'll become one of my readers and join my Reader News.

And, a big, huge thank you to my family, especially my awesome and amazing husband, Del, for all the support and encouragement! Thank you, thank you!

CHAPTER 1

*S*hanna Lyndley sat at her office desk, thumbing through her planner. The presentation was next Tuesday, which gave her exactly four more days. She had to nail this social media campaign if she had any hope of securing a senior account position at Rocky Mountain Public Relations.

Someone knocked at her office door.

"Come in," she said, keeping her gaze on her planner and mentally tallying how many hours she had. Stress weighed down her shoulders.

"Melanie Stringham confirmed the meeting on Tuesday," her assistant, Kaylie, said. She tucked a piece of her dark hair behind her ear. "And don't forget, you need to confirm your airline ticket so you can leave in," she paused and checked her watch, "an hour for the airport."

Shanna pushed out a breath, her anxiety building. "I'll do that right now." She pulled out her phone. "I don't have time to go to Amarillo for my parents' anniversary dinner. This couldn't be at a worse time. I need to prepare for the presentation on Tuesday."

"Your parents will be heartbroken if you don't go." Kaylie gave her a sympathetic look.

Shanna straightened in her chair. She'd have to figure out how to make it all work. "I know, I know. I wish it wasn't this weekend."

"It might be a nice getaway," Kaylie said brightly as she sat in the chair on the other side of the desk.

Shanna's phone buzzed. She read the text. "Oh, no." She slumped onto her desk.

"What is it?" Kaylie leaned forward.

"My flight has been canceled." How could this have happened? She was depending on that flight not only to get her back to Amarillo, but also to make adjustments to her presentation. Every minute counted, and Shanna couldn't afford to waste any precious time.

"What? Are you serious?" Kaylie's voice was filled with concern.

Shanna nodded. "Mechanical problems." *Great.* Now what was she going to do?

"Did they book you on another flight?"

Shanna scrolled down the screen of her phone, then gazed at Kaylie. "Doesn't look like it."

Pulling her brows together, Kaylie said, "They can't cancel the flight without giving you options."

"They can, apparently." Shanna tugged at her newly-lightened blond hair and wrapped a piece around her index finger.

Her phone buzzed again. "Oh, here's more info." Shanna read the text, then clicked over to a screen for the airline. "Looks like the next available flight is tomorrow afternoon. Not a lot of flights go to Amarillo from here, I guess." She clenched her jaw.

"Will that work?" Kaylie said, watching Shanna.

"I'd miss the brunch tomorrow, but I'd make it for the dinner and dance." Her mom had been planning this celebration for months and she wanted—*expected*—both Shanna and her brother, Patrick, to be there for all the events. Shanna's sister-in-law, Lacey, had been helping plan everything. Shanna couldn't miss it. She had to figure out what to do.

"That sounds like a good plan." Kaylie smiled.

Shanna sat back and closed her eyes for a moment. "You don't know my mom. This is a huge thing to her. I can't miss any of it."

Thinking about telling her mom she wouldn't be at the brunch made her break out in hives.

"What are you going to do?"

"I'll see if I can get another flight. But, for now, I have to go over my presentation and see if there are any last-minute things I need." Shanna had to pay attention to every detail.

"I'll help any way I can," Kaylie said, her brown eyes eager.

"Thanks. I appreciate it. If you can check on the images I sent you and proof them, that'd help." Shanna needed to make sure she didn't miss any specifics.

"I'm on it."

Kaylie left and Shanna made some notes. She'd been working for Rocky Mountain Public Relations for three years. This presentation would show her boss, Renae, that she was ready for a senior position. She didn't want to put too much pressure on herself, but since Dave Eddington was retiring next month, his position would be available.

Her phone buzzed. It was her mom. She braced herself, then said, "Hey, Mom."

"Hi, sweetie. I can't wait to see you in a few hours." Shanna could hear her mom's excitement.

Shanna bit her lip. She didn't want to disappoint her mom or listen to a lecture about attending family events. She inhaled, then said, "About that."

"What?" The alarm in her mom's voice was evident.

"My flight was canceled." She steeled herself for her mom's reaction.

"Canceled?" her mom said in a high-pitched voice. "For what reason?"

"Mechanical issues or something."

"That's ridiculous. Let me call them," her mom said with an indignant tone.

"Mom." Shanna shook her head. Her mother was a mover and a shaker, but even she wouldn't be able to convince an airline to fly a grounded plane. "I can take another flight," she said as calmly as possible, not wanting to tell her mom the next available flight wasn't until tomorrow.

"When? We have events planned." She didn't have to see her mom to know that her face was flushed with frustration.

"I'm going to look at flights as soon as we get off the phone."

"I hope you can get another one right away. I don't want you to miss anything. Lacey has done a fantastic job helping me get everything planned. You said you'd come all weekend. You haven't made a trip here in several months." Her mom was a master planner of guilt trips.

"I know. I'm sorry. I've been so busy at work." It was true. Shanna worked long hours trying to make a name for herself in Denver where she wasn't known as the daughter of Robert Lyndley, the mayor, the Chairman of the Chamber of Commerce, and a well-known business owner or Margot Lyndley, entrepreneur extraordinaire and owner of three popular florist shops.

"Get the earliest flight possible," her mom said in her familiar get-it-done-now tone.

"I'll see what I can do. I promise." Shanna wanted to be there, and she'd try her best to do that.

"I need both my children there for our big anniversary celebration. It'll mean so much to your father, too. Please be here as soon as possible," her mom said.

"I will." She hung up, then cradled her head in her hands. If only she had magical powers and could snap her fingers and instantly be in Amarillo.

"Uh, oh," Kaylie said as she walked in. "What happened?"

Shanna looked up. "My mom called."

Kaylie gave her a panicked expression. "Did you figure out a way to get to Amarillo?" She sat in the chair across the desk from Shanna.

"Not yet." Shanna scrolled on her phone. "I can't find any flights."

"What about a bus? When I was a kid, we used to take Greyhound to visit my grandparents. It wasn't that terrible. But it did take a long time. And it smelled like diesel." Kaylie appeared to be lost in her memories.

"No thanks," Shanna said, seeming to startle Kaylie back to reality.

"Maybe you could—" Kaylie started.

Shanna slapped her forehead. "I'll drive my car. It's only six hours or so. I can think about my presentation while I'm driving. That's the obvious answer." Why hadn't Shanna thought of this before? She could easily drive to Amarillo and be there late tonight, long before the festivities started tomorrow.

"Is it still making that noise?" Kaylie asked.

"Yeah, but I'm sure it isn't a big deal. My foreign car, as my dad likes to call it, has been very dependable, even if it is almost ten years old." Shanna had to defend her purchase of a Honda whenever she was around her dad, who owned a large Ford dealership.

"Road trip!" Kaylie raised her hands above her and pumped them.

"Wanna come?" If Shanna could convince Kaylie to come with her, she could get a lot of work done and kill two birds with one stone.

"Sounds fun, but I'm working at the restaurant tomorrow."

Shanna nodded. "One of these days, you'll get paid enough so you don't have to work shifts at Diego's." Once she had her promotion, she planned to put in a good word for Kaylie so she could get a raise.

Kaylie shrugged.

"If I leave by three o'clock, I can get home long before midnight. Then I'll be there for the brunch and all the festivities. Leave it to my mom to plan a huge, all-day production. Why do simple when extravagant will do?" Shanna laughed.

"Amarillo loves your dad."

"That's true." Shanna laughed.

"How can I help you get ready?" Kaylie clapped her hands together.

"I think I'm ready. I packed last night. I'll be back Sunday night. If you could pick up the materials from the printer Monday morning before you come in, that'd be great. Then I can go over everything." If it all went well, she'd be considered for Dave's position. At least she hoped so.

⁓

5

SHANNA DROVE BACK to her condo on the east side of Denver. She was proud of her first home purchase, even though her parents hadn't been in favor. She'd bought it last year before housing prices jumped up and she loved that it had been renovated so she could move right in.

She parked her car in her assigned stall, then strode across the sidewalk to her unit. She needed to change her clothes, grab her bags, and get some gas.

Changing into some yoga pants and a Dallas Cowboys t-shirt she'd had since high school, she found her bags, collected her toiletries, and grabbed an apple, a banana, and a protein drink from her refrigerator.

This would be such a quick trip she'd hardly be gone at all. She'd be back before she knew it and working toward her promotion.

CHAPTER 2

*C*ole Davis removed his cowboy hat and wiped the perspiration from his brow. He hung his hat on a peg next to the door. Making his way inside the Juniper Springs Inn, he noted that he needed to add some WD40 to the creaky hinge on the back door. He walked through the kitchen and over to the reservation desk where a man and woman were waiting. "Hi. Sorry about that. I was out back. I can check you in," he said, running his fingers through his hair to mask the hat head he was sure he had.

"This inn is lovely," the tall woman said. "You serve breakfast here?"

With a smile, he said, "Yes. Every morning beginning at seven. All homemade."

"It has some great reviews," the man with gray hair said.

"It's been in my family for three generations, and we try to make sure everyone who stays here feels like they're at home." He enjoyed welcoming new guests.

Cole retrieved the guest book. "Please sign in," he said as he placed the book down.

The woman took a pen from her purse. "I love the woodwork and the details, like the light fixtures. And even the pictures on the wall are reminiscent of the past. It makes me feel like I've stepped back in time."

"We like to keep things simple and appropriate for the time period when this was built. However, we are in the twenty-first century, so we do have Wi-Fi. It can be a little flaky at times. Your password is right here." He pointed to a sign on the desk. "We serve breakfast in there." He gestured to the dining room.

"Sounds wonderful." The woman gazed around.

Cole glanced at the book. "What brings you to Juniper Springs, Mr. and Mrs. Miller?"

"We wanted to recharge and slow down for the weekend," Mrs. Miller said with a smile.

Cole dipped his head. "This is a great place to do that." He handed them a key. "You'll be in the Columbine Room at the end of the hallway upstairs."

"Thank you." Mr. Miller grabbed the suitcase and his wife followed him upstairs.

As soon as the couple left, Cole's mom walked into the lobby area. "Billy has a school function for his daughter tonight. Would you mind being on-call for the tow truck?"

Cole shrugged. "Sure thing."

"Unless you have a date." Her eyes lit up.

Cole shook his head and smiled. Ever since he'd come home to help after his dad passed, his mom had been trying to fix him up with women, most of whom he'd either grown up with or watched grow up. Her last attempt was with a girl that was at least ten years younger, if not more. "Mom, I told you, I'm not here to date. I'm here to help you."

"Why can't you do both?" She looked through the guest book as if she weren't that interested in his answer.

"Dating isn't a priority." His last girlfriend, Melissa, had left such a sour taste in his mouth, he vowed to never date again.

His mom studied him. "Why?"

"Can we talk about something else?" He didn't want to rehash his love life with his mom. His phone vibrated and he pulled it from his pocket and looked at the text.

"Problem?" his mom asked as she stepped closer to him.

"No," he said. "I need to send in a file I've been working on."

"Are you sure the other lawyers aren't mad that you've been here so long?" It was the same question she kept asking, and Cole wasn't sure how else to reassure her.

"We've gone over this, Mom. I've been doing some work remotely with my computer. My boss is fine with it and so are my coworkers. They've all been understanding, because the most important thing is to help you with the businesses and the ranch." Cole placed his hands on his mom's shoulders. "Really."

"I worry. That's all," she said softly.

"I know. And I appreciate it. But you don't need to. I'm here as long as you need me." He wished he could take all her worries away.

Her eyes brimmed with tears. "I couldn't ask for a better son. Your dad would be so proud of you." She gave him a hug. "Thank you."

"You're very welcome."

She wiped at her eyes, then said, "I need to run to the store to get a few things for breakfast tomorrow. Can you watch the desk?"

He nodded. "I'll monitor calls for the tow truck in case anyone needs it." They didn't get many calls for towing, so he didn't expect to drive the truck.

His mom left and Cole looked over the bookings for the next few days.

"Hey, Cole," came a female voice.

His head snapped up. "Hi, Laurel." He smiled at the woman who was a few years younger.

"How are you?" She flipped her dark hair behind her shoulder as she walked around the reservation desk.

"Good. You?" He wanted to be polite even though he would rather have been talking to a rock outside than to Laurel.

"I'm wonderful now that I've seen you." She blinked her too-long eyelashes several times, making it obvious she was flirting with him.

"Are you looking for a room?" he said, trying to figure out why she was there.

She moved in closer to him, her strong perfume making him want to sneeze. "To share with you?"

"Uh, no." He stepped back. "I meant a room here at the inn." He wanted to make sure she didn't misunderstand him.

She giggled. "No, silly. I came in here specifically to see you before I go to work."

"Thanks. Uh, I appreciate that, but I'm so busy right now. I need to go check on the plumbing up in the Sky Room." He walked around her.

She turned and said, "I could come help you."

"Thanks, but I've got it." How much clearer did he need to be? Even if he were interested in dating someone, which he definitely wasn't, it wouldn't be Laurel. He wasn't attracted to her even one iota.

Her shoulders slumped, but then she brightened. "How about going to dinner now? Or we could watch a movie at my place."

He held his hand up. "Thanks, but, like I said before, I'm not interested in dating anyone right now. I'm only here helping my mom until she can run everything on her own and then I need to get back to my law practice." He'd already told her this several times. Why wouldn't she get it?

She placed her hand on his arm. "But we could have so much fun together."

He nodded and moved away from her. "I appreciate the invitation, but I—"

"Well, I'm not going to give up." She smiled and then turned and left.

After the door shut, his cousin, Madi, said, "She's beautiful, why don't you want to go out with her?"

"Where did you come from?" He hadn't seen her come in.

"The kitchen." She smiled. "Why don't you want to go out with her?"

Cole shrugged. "Not interested."

"Because your last girlfriend was a lyin' cheater who broke your heart?" Madi plopped on a chair next to the desk, then took a bite of the apple she held in her hand.

"Who told you that?" Cole said.

"Aunt Belle."

Cole shook his head. "Don't you need to clean some rooms or help bake for tomorrow's breakfast or something?" He didn't want to talk about Melissa. Or why they broke up. He didn't want to talk about any woman ever again.

Madi smiled, then jumped up from her chair and scurried off.

Cole wished everyone would stay out of his love life. He was perfectly happy being single. He planned to help his mom until she felt confident running the businesses on her own. Then he'd return to Fort Collins and to his law practice. He didn't need female companionship to do any of that.

"Hello," said a woman with red hair and wearing wire-framed glasses as she walked in.

"Hi. Can I help you?" Cole made his way back to the reservation desk.

"I'm here to check in. My husband is bringing in our bags." She set her purse down.

"Can I get your name?"

"Carolyn Branson."

"Here it is," Cole said, opening the guest book. "If you'll sign here, I'll get your key. I think you'll like the John Wayne Room."

"John Wayne, huh?" she said with a raised eyebrow.

"My dad was a big fan and he wanted to name a room after him." Memories of watching John Wayne movies with his dad washed over him and reminded him of his loss.

"My husband loves his movies too. He'll be right at home," she said, jerking Cole from his thoughts.

"That's what we hope." Cole enjoyed being an attorney, but he also enjoyed helping people feel at home in the inn.

"We're excited to stay here," she said. "My sister came last year and raved about it, especially the delicious breakfast."

Cole nodded. He was happy that the inn had such a good reputation. He was sure his father, grandfather, and great-grandfather would all be glad to hear that. "Let me know if you need anything." He handed her a key.

After the Bransons went upstairs, Cole made his way to the Sky room to see if he could fix the clog in the drain.

CHAPTER 3

*S*hanna adjusted the volume in her car stereo so she could listen to a podcast. "Time Finder" was one of her favorites for learning how to make more time in the day and be more productive. She needed this desperately if she wanted to get ahead and someday have her own public relations firm. *Productivity* was her word for the year, and she was doing all she could to accomplish more each day.

"Remember, planning is important. You can squeeze more time out of the day if you plan it and then stick to your plan no matter what. The most successful people don't veer from their agenda. You can start small but be protective of your schedule. You won't get ahead if you let things continue to derail you. You are in charge of you and your time. Make time work for you," Alanna Brewster, the most popular time management guru, said.

Shanna nodded vigorously. All she had to do was organize her time more efficiently to get more done. She planned to use any down time to dedicate to her upcoming presentation to Wendolin Hotels and Resorts. The company was looking to reinvigorate its image and appeal to a younger audience to attract them to its various resorts in

Colorado. It was a big account and if she aced the presentation, she felt confident she'd move up to the senior position.

In her mind, she went through the checklist of things she still needed to do to make her presentation unforgettable.

Since it was almost the middle of June, the sun wouldn't set for a few hours still. She was glad she'd be traveling in daylight for most of the trip because she didn't enjoy driving at night.

It was a breathtaking drive with some of the most exquisite mountains lining the highway. The highest peaks were still capped with snow. If only she had time to stop and explore. But she didn't. She needed to get to Amarillo, attend the festivities for her parents, and hop right back into her car to get home to Denver. This had to be a quick, uneventful trip.

She continued to listen to past episodes of her favorite time-saving podcasts when her car started to make a strange sound. There wasn't any smoke, but the temperature gauge was rising.

"Oh, no," she said aloud. "I don't have time for any car problems." She patted the dashboard. "Come on. You can keep going."

A few more miles and the car was still making a noise and the temperature gauge indicated the engine was even hotter. She pulled over by a rest stop and called her dad, even though she knew he'd censure her about owning a Honda instead of a Ford. He knew cars and she needed his expertise.

"Hello?" came his familiar deep voice.

"Daddy, my car is acting funny." She tried not to sound panicky.

"What does that mean?" he asked.

"It seems really hot and it's making a noise." She tapped the temperature gauge on the dashboard.

"What kind of noise?"

"I don't know. A weird one." How could she describe it?

"That's not very descriptive."

"It's kind of whining or moaning. I don't know. It doesn't sound right. What should I do?" She massaged her temples.

"Are you close to a town?" he asked.

She tried to recall what signs she'd seen. She wasn't paying much attention because she'd been focused on the podcast. "I think I saw a sign for some kind of springs a while back." All she could see was the road with some fields on either side of it and mountains in the background.

"I'm not sure what's wrong, but I think it would be best to call for a tow," he said.

"Seriously?" Shanna wanted to scream. A tow? This wasn't what she'd planned. "What am I going to do?"

"Stay calm," he said. "It could be something like your water pump."

"Is that hard to fix?" she asked, feeling anything but calm.

"It depends."

Shanna let out a long breath then rested her head against the steering wheel. "I need to be home tonight so I can be there tomorrow morning for all your anniversary events. Mom will be so upset if I'm not there."

"Let's not worry about that right now. Why don't you call for a tow? Any repair shops will probably be closed for the night, but maybe you can check early in the morning." His voice was reassuring.

"Maybe it'll be a quick fix and I'll make it there in time for the brunch. I'm about halfway," she said, trying to be optimistic.

"Let me know what happens," he said.

"I will."

"Don't you worry. I can come get you if I need to." She could almost feel her dad's arm around her shoulder, making her feel better.

"It'll be fine." She appreciated his willingness to come get her, but she was a grown woman with a real job, and she needed to figure it all out. "Thanks, Daddy."

After she hung up, she pulled up her browser. Thankfully, she had cell service even though she seemed to be in a pretty remote area. Shanna had driven this route before but hadn't paid attention. She was always eager to get to her destination without much regard to the journey from one point to the next. When she typed "towing near me" into the search bar on her phone, Davis Towing popped up.

She clicked on the phone number. It rang a few times.

"Hello?" said a man's voice.

She cleared her throat. "Yes, is this Davis Towing?"

"It is."

"Hi. I'm stuck out here on the highway by a rest stop. My car is making a weird sound and it's really hot." Shanna didn't want to sound too panicked even though that was the way she felt.

"Your car is really hot?" His tone sounded almost humorous, but there was nothing funny about this situation.

"Yes. My car. The temperature gauge is in the red. I was afraid to keep driving it."

"All right. We don't want your car to overheat. Sounds like it could be the water pump or the radiator," he said.

"Can you come and tow it to a repair shop?" The sooner she could get it towed, the sooner she could solve the problem and get back on her way to Amarillo.

"Yes, ma'am."

"Can you come now?" She didn't want to seem too pushy, but she was desperate. There was no time in her plan to waste on car repairs. This would tank her productivity for the weekend, not to mention make her mom flip out if she didn't make it for the celebration. Shanna didn't like either of those two scenarios.

"Yes, ma'am," he said again.

"Thank you. Please, hurry. I need to get my car fixed so I can get to Amarillo for my parents' anniversary celebration. It's very important for me to be there." Maybe if she explained her predicament and appealed to his sympathy, he'd make an extra effort to help her.

"Can you tell me where you are?" he asked.

"Uh, on the road." Obviously, she was on the highway.

"There are a lot of roads, ma'am. I'll need you to be more specific." She wasn't sure, but she felt like he was making fun of her.

"Oh. I'm on I-25, but I'm in the middle of nowhere. I'm driving to Amarillo from Denver." Hopefully, that was specific enough.

"Any idea how many miles from Juniper Springs?"

How was she supposed to know that? This tow truck driver was beginning to annoy her. "Can I just drop you a pin?"

"This is a landline, ma'am."

"Wait. What? There are still landlines?" Who even had a landline these days? Did she enter some portal and go back in time? And she wished he'd stop calling her ma'am. It made her feel like she was an old lady.

"Yes, ma'am. We still have landlines here."

Wherever *here* was, it was stuck in the past. No matter, she needed to get her car towed and repaired. She hoped that would be possible in a place that still had landlines. "I'm not sure where I am. I haven't seen any signs for a while. Can you please just come?"

"All right. I'll start driving north of town and look for you," he said in a pleasant enough voice.

"Thank you." She gazed around her surroundings. "Oh, I'm at a rest stop."

"That makes it easier. You're ten miles out of town," he said.

"See you soon?" She hoped it wouldn't take too long for him to get there.

"Yes, ma'am."

She ended the call and stared at her phone. Of all the times for her car to break down, this was the worst one. She had the presentation looming over her and her parents' big party—why did her car have to do this right now?

Trying to make the best use of her time—as her time management gurus suggested—Shanna listened to another podcast on her phone. After thirty minutes, she was antsy. Why wasn't the tow truck guy there yet? Did people move extra slow in this area? When would he be there? Was he even coming?

Daylight gave way to dusk as she sat in her car. She decided to call the towing company again and try to explain her urgency as politely as possible.

"Hello?" came the same voice. *Oh, great, he hasn't even left yet.*

"It's me, again, Shanna. The one with the broken-down car by the rest stop. You said you'd come a long time ago. Why haven't you left yet?" She was trying to be patient.

"I have left." He sounded a little miffed.

"But you said this was a landline," she said, defending herself.

"That I forwarded to my cell."

"Oh." She felt sheepish.

"I'm about five minutes from your location," he said, matter-of-factly.

"Thank you." She didn't want to be rude, she simply wanted him to tow her car so she could get it fixed and be on her way. Time was not on her side.

She ended the call. He sounded like he was probably middle-aged, balding, with a belly, and a wad of chewing tobacco in his lip whose life revolved around towing cars. The sooner she could be done with this whole experience, the better.

When the truck pulled up, she squinted at the headlights. She unbuckled herself from her seat and exited her car. She waited for him to exit his truck.

The door opened and he stepped out from behind it and started to walk toward her. She swallowed back all her assumptions.

Even in the dusky light she could see he was not middle-aged. He had no belly whatsoever. No wad in his mouth. And if he was balding, she couldn't tell because he was wearing a light-colored cowboy hat. He was tall and trim and wore his jeans and t-shirt well. In fact, he looked like he'd stepped out of a magazine shoot for one of those hot cowboy calendars. Her heart skittered as he approached.

"Ms. Shanna, I believe?" he said. He dipped his head.

"Uh, yes, that's me." She tried to keep her composure, wishing she was dressed in something more attractive than her yoga pants and oversized t-shirt.

"Cole Davis." He stuck out his hand.

As she slid her hand into his, she couldn't deny the jolt of energy she felt. She quickly withdrew her hand. "Thank you for coming."

"Yes, ma'am."

Hearing him say it while he was standing there, his dark hair peeking out from under his hat, was much more endearing than it had been on the phone.

"Any chance you fix cars?" Shanna didn't want to be distracted by his appearance. She needed to get her car fixed. And fast.

"My family owns the repair shop in town. Davis Garage." He adjusted his hat.

She nodded. "So you fix cars?"

"Not personally anymore. But I used to all through high school." He smiled and she ignored the butterfly that knocked against the walls of her stomach.

"Do you think it'll be fixed in the morning?" She wanted him to know what she expected.

"Jimmy Bob is our mechanic now. He's a good one. But it'll depend on if it needs any parts. And if his wife is having the baby." He laughed, then walked to the other side of the car. "I need to hook the car up so I can tow it."

Shanna stood out of the way while he worked. She tried not to notice the muscles that flexed in his arms while he hooked up the car within the glow of the light on the back of his truck.

After fifteen minutes or so, Mr. Hot Cowboy said, "I think it's all ready."

Shanna glanced around. How would she get to the town?

Seeming to sense her question, he said, "You can ride in the cab with me."

"Oh, yeah. I'm glad you aren't going to make me walk." She let out a nervous laugh.

"If you'd rather walk, you can." He shrugged.

"Uh, no. Thanks." Did that mean he didn't want to drive her? Why was she worried about that? She needed to get herself together. This tow truck driver might be handsome and might possibly be affecting her—slightly—but she needed to focus on getting her car repaired as soon as possible—that was all that mattered. And if she repeated it to herself enough times, she'd remember it.

She climbed up into the cab. When he got in, she caught a whiff of spearmint mixed with a faint woodsy scent that made her think of autumn. He turned and looked at her, which made her heart do a flippy thing in her chest. "Buckle up," he said. "Please."

19

She pressed her seatbelt into the latch, reprimanding herself for having any sort of reaction to this man. Why did she feel so drawn to him? It was ridiculous. *Stay focused on the car, not the man.* "I can't believe my car broke down. I wasn't planning on that," she said weakly.

"Usually, people don't plan on their car breaking down." He laughed as he pulled out onto the highway towing her car.

She wanted to give herself a facepalm. "Well, yeah. Obviously. I only mean it's *really* important for me to be in Amarillo before eleven a.m. tomorrow."

"What happens then?" It seemed like a sincere question.

"It's a brunch." She smoothed her hair and relaxed a bit in the seat.

"Must be an important brunch for you to drive all the way from Denver for it." He adjusted his rearview mirror.

"It's for my parents. It's their thirtieth wedding anniversary tomorrow. We have a brunch and then some other activities followed by a dinner and dance. My mom has been planning it for many months." Although it was during a stressful time at work, Shanna didn't want to miss it.

"Sounds like a great celebration. Thirty years is a long time." He gave her a sideways glance.

"Yeah. My dad was mayor of Amarillo for two terms, and he was the chairman of the Chamber of Commerce, so a lot of people know him. I think he wants to run for state government." Her father hadn't officially declared his candidacy, but he'd talked about it frequently.

He nodded. "Did you grow up in Amarillo?"

"Yes. Born and raised there." The conversation seemed to flow easily.

"You left it for Denver?" he asked.

Feeling more at ease, she said, "Growing up with such a well-known family was hard. Everyone saw me as Robert Lyndley's daughter. Plus, my mom owns three floral shops." She gazed out the window. "Going to Denver was my chance to forge my own path apart from my family. I wanted to prove to myself I could be successful." She hadn't meant to share so much personal information, but something about him made her feel safe. "Patrick stayed in Amarillo and works for my dad at the car dealership."

"Patrick?"

"Oh, he's my older brother. He's married with two super cute boys." Thinking of her energetic nephews warmed her heart.

Cole nodded.

Shanna coughed. "Now, that I've told you my life story, what about you? Are you from . . . here?" She wasn't sure where *here* was.

"Juniper Springs," he said, keeping his gaze on the road and smiling.

"That's a nice name for a city." Though she'd driven between Denver and Amarillo before, she'd never noticed any of the places along the route. She'd always been in a hurry.

"I'd call it more of a town." He laughed. "It's small."

"Oh. A small town." She'd only lived in cities.

"But yes. I'm from Juniper Springs. My family has been here for a few generations. We own the garage and tow truck as well as a bed and breakfast called the Juniper Springs Inn." He glanced at her. "Pretty original name, huh?" He laughed. "We also run cattle on our land."

Shanna glanced at the man driving the truck. "You're a real, live cowboy?"

He dipped his head. "In the flesh."

"I've never met a cowboy." She studied him. "What do you do, exactly?"

He shrugged a shoulder. "Keep track of all the cattle, help deliver any that are having problems, brand them after they're born. Haul them to the sale barn. Take care of any that get sick. You know, watch over all of them. Oh, and fix fences. Keep up the pasture. Make sure they've got water."

"Sounds . . . interesting." Shanna had never thought about taking care of cattle. She bought meat at the grocery store and that's about as far as it went.

Cole adjusted his hat. "*Interesting*. That's a good word for it."

Shanna looked in the side mirror trying to get a glimpse of her car. "I really hope we can get my car fixed as soon as possible."

"Like I said, Jimmy Bob will be in. Unless his wife is having the baby."

"But he's not the only mechanic. Is he?" Surely, there were others at this car repair shop.

"He is." Cole glanced down at the dashboard, then back through the windshield.

Trying not to freak out, she said, "But you could look at it?"

"I could but—"

"Please. I need to get back on the road. I want to be at my parents' celebration, but I also need to get back to Denver for a big presentation on Tuesday. A presentation that's super important to my career." The familiar stress headache started to form.

He glanced at her. "Seems like you're pretty keyed up."

"I guess. If you call wanting to make my parents happy by attending their anniversary celebration at the worst time at work, and then making sure everything is in order so I can wow the owner of a big resort with a social media campaign, so I can then be considered for a senior position keyed up. Then, yeah. I'm keyed up." She drew in a big breath.

"Do you ever take time to relax? You know, enjoy life?"

She guffawed. As if there was ever time to relax. "I'm interested in productivity. In fact, on this drive I didn't want to waste any time, so I've listened to podcasts on how to make more time in my day to get more done."

He shrugged. "I get that."

"You do?" She gazed at him. He didn't seem the type to be worried about being productive. How many cows did he need to take care of anyway?

After several moments, he said, "I was fully immersed in the rat race."

She blinked. "You were? Here?" There was a rat race in this small town? With the cows?

"No, no." He waved his hand. "In Fort Collins, actually." He slipped her a glance.

She jerked her head back. "Wait, you live in Fort Collins?"

"Yes."

She was confused. "So are you here visiting and, what? Decided to drive the tow truck for fun?" She laughed.

An expression crossed his face and she suddenly felt like she'd said something wrong.

Licking his lips, he said, "I came back to Juniper Springs to help after my dad passed."

"Oh, I'm so sorry," Shanna said softly, feeling like she was an inch tall.

"Thanks. It's been hard, but we're getting through it." He checked his side mirror.

Shanna glanced at her hands in her lap and didn't say anything for a few minutes for fear there wouldn't be enough room in her mouth for both of her feet.

He broke the silence. "I was so busy with my law practice I didn't come home to visit much. I was too preoccupied with winning cases and getting ahead. When my dad passed, I regretted being too busy. I'd let time slip by in the name of success. I resolved that it was time for a slower pace. A pace that allowed me to enjoy life and, even more, enjoy the people I love. I can't get back the time I missed with my dad, but I can spend more time with my mom."

Shanna blinked. This guy was different from her. While she could understand his feelings after his dad died, she didn't want slower. She loved her fast-paced lifestyle in the city. She hadn't been home to see her parents in quite a while, but she was making a name for herself. Shanna had no regrets.

They pulled up to a red steel building with large garage doors. "Here we are," he said. "I'll unhook your car."

"Thank you for towing it."

He smiled and even in the dim light of the truck her stomach flip-flopped, which irritated her. She'd barely met this man and she was in no way attracted to him. At all. He seemed nice enough, but she'd never date him for so many reasons. She must be exhausted and that's why she reacted this way.

After he unhooked her car, he came back to the tow truck. "I can let you sleep in the truck, but I think you'd be more comfortable at our bed and breakfast." He winked and, again, her stomach turned upside down. *Stupid stomach.*

"Oh, yeah, I guess I'll need to find a place to stay for the night." She hadn't even thought of that.

"I'm happy to take you to any hotel." He puffed out a laugh. "Hmm, that came out wrong."

She snickered behind closed lips. "I'd love to see the bed and breakfast your family owns." She imagined it was a quaint, comfortable place.

"I think we have a room available. My truck is over here." He pointed to a big, shiny black truck with silver hubcaps. If she ever owned a truck, which she didn't expect she would, she'd own one like this. She wanted to tell him it was a pretty truck but thought better of it.

Shanna exited the tow truck and they walked over to his Ford F-350. "Nice," she said.

"I'm a fan of Ford trucks." He removed his hat and ran his fingers through his thick, dark hair, then replaced his hat.

"My dad will be pleased. I mean, not that he'll ever meet you or anything. I simply mean he'd be pleased to know anyone likes Ford trucks. Because he owns a dealership. A Ford dealership. In Amarillo." She shook her head slightly at the words that fell so awkwardly out of her mouth.

They drove to the inn, a red brick building that appeared to have been an older home in its previous life. "This is lovely," she said as she stepped inside, feeling like she'd traveled back to the old west.

"It was built in 1880 for the town's richest family. My great-grandfather bought it in 1933. It was run down and needed many repairs. He did the repairs himself and turned it into a boarding house that then transformed into a bed and breakfast when my father took it over in the late eighties."

"It's beautiful. I've driven between Denver and Amarillo before, but I never noticed this town. I guess I was always in such a rush." Maybe she had missed a few things in her fevered attempt to use up every second of the day.

He smiled and in the brighter light of the room, she noticed a dimple on his left cheek. She shook it from her mind. Dimples could be dangerous.

"Hello," an older woman with short, salt-and-pepper hair said.

"Hi, Mom. This is Shanna." Cole gestured to Shanna.

"Ah, the stranded driver outside of town?" The woman gave a genuine smile and Shanna noticed the crinkles that formed by her eyes.

"Yes. That's me. Stranded driver." It wasn't a title she wanted.

Cole walked around the desk and looked over a book. "She needs to stay the night until Jimmy Bob can get to her car in the morning."

"We have the River Room available," his mom said. "Madi cleaned it earlier."

"River Room?" Shanna said.

"It overlooks the Willow River," Cole said. "A popular room that my cousin cleaned for you it seems."

Shanna couldn't help but grin. "Sounds nice. And you have Wi-Fi?"

A smile slid across his mom's face and landed on a dimple on her left cheek, same as Cole. "Usually."

"Oh." *Usually* wasn't what she wanted to hear associated with Wi-Fi.

"It can be a bit finicky at times," the woman said while she waved her hand. "Nothing to lose sleep over."

"I'm sure it will be fine. I have a presentation to deliver at work on Tuesday and I was planning to get some work done this weekend." She had to be productive and get things done, which was her mantra, and she was sticking to it.

"During your parents' celebration?" Cole gazed at her with his head tilted to one side.

Feeling embarrassed, she said, "During the downtime. Not during the actual celebration." Why did she feel the need to explain this to a complete stranger?

He nodded. "You might be able to get access to the internet tonight. It usually works later at night when not so many people are on it."

"Have you eaten supper?" his mom asked.

"No." As if on cue, Shanna's stomach began to rumble. She'd had snacks, but she was still hungry.

"Oh, well, you must go to Ada's Diner. She makes the best chicken and dumpling soup." His mom wrapped her arm around Shanna's shoulders as if they'd been lifelong friends. Surprisingly, the gesture felt warm and natural.

"Isn't it too late?" Shanna assumed such a small town closed early every night.

The woman patted Shanna's arm. "No, not at all. I'll give her a call and let her know you'll be there soon. Cole, you wouldn't mind taking our visitor over, would you?" she asked.

"I don't want to be any trouble." Shanna didn't want to impose.

"No trouble at all. Right, son?" she said while nodding.

"Right." Cole shifted his weight.

"Let's get you checked in and up to your room first. Oh, and by the way, my name is Anabelle, but my friends all call me Belle. You let me know if you need anything at all."

"Thank you," Shanna said. Belle was so friendly and welcoming. She'd never been treated like this at a hotel. It was almost as if she were a long-lost member of the family.

Shanna made her way up the stairs.

"MOTHER." Cole gave her an I-know-what-you're-trying-to-do look.

"Yes?" she said with a coy expression.

His mom was so transparent. "Stop doing what you're doing."

"Whatever do you mean?" she said, her eyes full of mischief.

"You know what I mean." She could play dumb all she wanted, but he knew exactly what she was up to.

"Cole, honey. This young woman is stranded in a strange town. Don't you think the neighborly thing to do is to get her some dinner and make her feel comfortable?" She said it so convincingly.

He narrowed his eyes. "The *neighborly* thing?"

"Of course. What other reason could there be?" She straightened a pillow on the chair by the desk.

"Don't think you're fooling me any." He wanted her to know that he saw right through her.

She clutched at her chest with feigned innocence. "I clearly have no idea what you are implying."

Cole shook his head and walked back to the kitchen to get a drink of water. He didn't like it when his mother tried to play matchmaker, especially when she was so obvious.

Why would she try to match him up with a woman who would be gone in less than a day? A woman who was as different from him as Denver was from Juniper Springs. Besides, he'd told his mom after this last break-up that he wasn't interested in a relationship with any woman. He wanted to focus on helping her get back on her feet and that was it.

"Cole?" His cousin, Madi, broke into his thoughts, jarring him back to reality.

He turned and gazed at her. "Yeah?"

"Where were you?" Madi said, jumping up and sitting on the counter.

"Uh, right here." He held his hands out in front of him. "In the kitchen."

Pointing at him she said, "Um, no. You were definitely somewhere else."

He scowled at her and reached into the cabinet to grab a glass.

"Aunt Belle said you're taking a guest over to the diner." She twisted her long dark hair into a messy bun on top of her head.

Cole rolled his eyes.

"What?" she said.

"My mom is trying to play matchmaker." He filled his glass with some water.

"She is?" Madi leaned toward him and clasped her hands. "Tell me more."

"There is no more to tell." He guzzled his water.

"Except that you're taking a woman out," Madi said with a wide grin.

"No." He held up his hand. "This isn't some kind of date. I gave her a ride into town because I towed her car to the garage. Mom told her she should go to Ada's and that I'd take her."

Madi started chuckling.

He set his glass on the counter. "Glad you find this amusing."

"What will it hurt?" She jumped down from the counter. "You take her to the diner and then you never see her again."

"Exactly." He was glad Madi understood.

With a crinkled nose, Madi said, "Huh?"

"What's the point?"

Madi studied him. "Oh, I get it."

Cole shifted his weight and then pushed out a breath. "You get what?"

Nodding, Madi said, "You like her."

"I *like* her? What am I? In third grade? Should I send her a love note? Let her check yes or no?" He shook his head dismissively. Both Madi and his mom were irritating him.

Madi circled him. "You can deny it all you want, but I can see it. You're attracted to her."

Tired of this conversation, Cole said, "You got me."

"I'm serious." She placed her hands on her hips.

"Look, Madi, I know you're a hopeless romantic. But I'm a realist. I'm not interested in this woman, or any woman for that matter. I've had enough bad dating experiences to last me a lifetime." How much clearer could he be?

"So you're gonna be a bachelor, like, forever?" she asked with an arched eyebrow.

"Why not?" It sounded like a better plan than getting his heart ripped out and shredded by a two-timing . . . He'd been there, done that. More than once. No way was he about to do it again.

"I think you like this woman. Maybe you should stop judging the present by the past." She patted him on the shoulder. "Just a thought."

After Madi left the kitchen, Cole leaned against the counter. He was not interested in a woman he'd barely met. How many ways could he say that?

Sure, her blue eyes drew him in, and her silky blond hair was nice. She smelled good--like flowers on a spring morning. But she was virtually a stranger, and probably like all the other women he'd known. A cheater.

Besides, tomorrow she'd be on her way out of Juniper Springs. That would be the end of it.

CHAPTER 4

*a*fter freshening up a bit, Shanna made her way back downstairs to the lobby. She didn't need anyone to take her to the diner. She was perfectly capable of doing that herself, but when Cole appeared through the doorway wearing that same cowboy hat and smiled, she had to admit that going with him wasn't the worst idea.

"Oh, hi," Belle said from behind the desk. "Cole is ready to take you. Ada said she's expecting you."

"Thank you. That's very kind." She appreciated Belle thinking of her.

Belle approached her with a sympathetic expression. "Car problems are no fun at all. Ada's cooking will help you forget your troubles." She touched Shanna on the arm. "And my son is a great companion."

Shanna bit back a smile. Was this endearing woman trying to fix her up with Cole? She did realize that Shanna was only here momentarily, right? As soon as her car was fixed, she was headed out of town. "Thanks."

"My mother thinks a lot of my conversational skills." He walked closer to her and she smelled a whiff of spearmint. "I'm happy to take you over to Ada's," he said.

"Thanks." She was grateful for his kindness.

"After you," he said as he opened the front door of the inn. Shanna walked through the doorway and out onto the sidewalk looking for his truck.

Cole started walking.

"Wait. We're not driving?"

He turned back to her. "It's a nice evening, and the diner isn't too far. Unless you'd rather drive?"

"A walk, huh?" Shanna didn't take many opportunities to walk anywhere. Life in Denver was one big rush, which she loved. She didn't like to have downtime because she felt like she was wasting time that she could be using to get things done.

"Sometimes it's nice to slow down and take the scenic route," he said as if reading her thoughts.

"Because that's your philosophy. That's what you've missed about Juniper Springs—a slower pace."

"You are an excellent listener." He seemed pleased that she remembered their conversation in the tow truck.

She smiled.

"Until recently, my life was scheduled from morning to night. Meetings with clients, pro bono work, volunteer work, studying new cases and laws. I was spinning so many plates," he said.

"Then your dad passed."

He nodded, then gazed out ahead of them. "You think your parents will live forever. When you lose one, you realize that time isn't your friend. Once it's gone, it's gone. You can't ever get it back."

Though he had a point about not being able to get time back, Cole thought of time so differently than she did. Shanna wanted to use every minute of every day. She didn't have time to slow down.

Cole fanned his hand out. "Here we are at Ada's." He opened the creaky wooden door and gestured for Shanna to go inside.

A round woman with bleached blond hair and rosy cheeks said, "Ah, you must be Shanna."

"Yes."

31

Ada grabbed her into a bear hug and Shanna didn't know what to do. "Good to meet you."

"Uh, you, too," Shanna said with uneasiness. She wasn't used to strangers hugging her.

"And Cole. How are you, hon?" She gave him a hug.

"Good to see you Aunt Ada," Cole said with a grin.

Shanna looked at him. "She's your aunt?"

"Not technically," Ada said with a flourish. "But I've known this boy all his life and I've diapered that bottom so many times—"

"All right, all right." He held his hands up. "We don't need to go into that. Ada and my mom have been friends for many years."

"And I never had any of my own kids, so I adopted Cole." She swung her arm around him. "Now, come sit down and have a good meal. Belle says your car broke down."

Shanna nodded as they sat at a table with a vase of fake pink flowers. News traveled fast in this tiny town. "I'm hoping to get it fixed quickly."

"Jimmy Bob is a great mechanic," Ada said. "He's been working on cars since he was this high." She motioned with her hand indicating a small size.

"I've heard he's very good." Shanna glanced at Cole.

"What can I get you?" Ada pulled a pencil from behind her ear and grabbed a pad of paper from her pocket.

Trying to fit in, Shanna said, "Belle recommended your chicken and dumpling soup."

"Ah, yes. That's her favorite." She studied Shanna for a moment. "But I think you might be more of a chef salad kind of a gal."

"I do like salads."

"Women always like salads," Cole said.

"Cole would know, too, because he's known a lot of women." Ada gave a belly laugh and then clapped him on the shoulder.

"Is that so?" Shanna said, giving him a once over. She hadn't pegged him for a womanizer.

"Oh yeah," Ada said enthusiastically. "He's the heart breaker in this neck of the woods."

Cole cleared his throat. "Okay, Aunt Ada, can I get a Juniper Burger?"

"What kind of hamburger is that?" Shanna asked.

"It's a one-quarter pounder with lettuce, tomatoes, and home-made dill pickles. Plus, my secret sauce," Ada said with obvious pride.

"Hmm. That sounds delicious. I'll have one of those." Shanna nodded.

Cole gave her a surprised look.

"I love hamburgers even more than salads," she said in a satisfied tone.

A teenager with curly brown hair came to the table with two glasses of water. "Hey, Cole," he said as he set the glasses down.

"How's your mom, Nate?" Cole asked.

"Doing okay. She went back to work last week." Nate placed a couple of napkins on the table.

"Did you get another car?" Cole said, a sympathetic look in his blue eyes.

"Yeah, my uncle gave us one of his."

"Glad to hear she's recovering," Cole said. It was easy to see that he cared about this boy.

"She says her arm is still sore, but she can stock shelves at Wrigleys." Nate nodded. "Let me know if you need anything else," he said, then left.

"Wrigleys?" Shanna said. She'd never heard of that store.

"It's our local grocery store. Nate's mom, Sara, has worked there since his father left town." He took a sip of his water. "She had a car accident a while back when a deer ran out in front of her, and she swerved to miss it. Ran right into a fence and totaled the car. The deer was fine, but Sara got hurt."

"Oh." Even though she'd never met Nate or his mom, Shanna felt bad for both of them.

"Nate's a nice kid. Got into a little trouble a year or so back but Ada took him under her wing, and he seems to be doing well now." He took another sip of water.

Shanna blinked. "This town is so different from anywhere I've lived."

"You mean where hardly anyone knows anyone else?"

"Yeah." She nodded.

"Everyone here knows everyone *and* all their business," he said with a laugh.

Shanna nodded again. She knew the gossip mill all too well from the time her dad was mayor.

"But it's like we're all family," Cole said. "Something I've missed since I've been gone."

"I don't think I could do a small town like this. No offense, but I think I'd feel suffocated." She took a sip of cold water.

Ada brought out their hamburgers, a scent of onions and char-broiled meat trailing her. Shanna had never seen such a huge burger.

"I hope you're hungry," Cole said.

Shanna gazed directly at him, feeling challenged. "You don't think I can finish this?"

He shrugged. "Well . . ."

"All right. Game on. I can finish this easy," she said with big words she wasn't sure she could support.

Cole smirked. "I'll be shocked if you can eat half that burger. It's almost as big as you are."

Shanna inhaled a deep breath, then sunk her teeth into the soft, homemade bun and the thick, juicy patty. As she finished the bite and sat back, she could feel a dribble of liquid slip down her chin. Before she could do anything, Cole handed her a napkin.

"These burgers are definitely napkin worthy. You'll need a few of these." He winked and handed her some more napkins.

With warmed cheeks, she wiped at her mouth. It was a good thing she wasn't trying to impress this guy, because otherwise she'd be mortified that she had burger juice oozing out of her mouth.

"Good?" he said with a smile that made her heartbeat jump.

"Yeah. Very good." She dabbed at her mouth again. "What's in the secret sauce?" She couldn't quite place the taste.

He gave her a look.

"What?"

He cupped his hand to his mouth. "If we knew, it wouldn't be a secret sauce," he whispered.

"Yeah, but I'm sure people know." There was no way this sauce was actually a secret.

He shook his head. "Ada guards the ingredients like they're a matter of national security. She says it's what keeps people coming back for her burgers."

Shanna took another juicy bite. This had to be the best burger she'd had in a long time. Maybe ever. Ada certainly knew how to make delectable hamburgers. While Shanna loved salads, she was always a sucker for a good burger. And this one would be at the top of her list.

Cole's phone buzzed. He looked at the screen. "It's Jimmy Bob."

"But the shop was closed when we left my car there."

"I asked him to swing by real quick and have a look for you since you're in a hurry." He said it as if it was no big deal.

Shanna was touched by Cole's thoughtfulness.

"Hey, Jimmy Bob. . . yeah . . . thanks for going over . . . it is? You're sure? . . . Can you get it done tomorrow? . . . All right . . . let me know . . .Thanks, bye." He ended the call.

Shanna shut her eyes. "Okay, give me the news."

"Don't you want to open your eyes?" he said.

"Nope." She squeezed her eyes tighter.

"Really?"

Keeping her eyes closed, she explained, "If I squeeze my eyes really tight, the news won't be as bad."

"I've never heard of that." She could hear the disbelief in his voice.

"My brother and I devised it," she said, nodding.

"Okay, then."

"What's the news?" she asked, preparing herself as best she could.

"Jimmy Bob said it's the water pump. Good thing you pulled over when you did."

"Can he fix it?" That was what was most important. She needed the car fixed pronto.

"Yes," Cole said.

"Tomorrow?" *Please say he can fix it tomorrow.*

"Look, I can't keep talking to you with your eyes shut like this. Can you open them? Please?" Cole said.

"I guess." She reluctantly lifted her lids.

"He said that if the water pump is in stock, he can have it fixed tomorrow." Cole munched on a French fry.

"Oh, this is wonderful news. See, the squeezing eye thing actually works." What a relief he could fix her car tomorrow. She'd be back on the road and there for the celebration.

"That's *if* it's in stock." He looked at her as if to make sure she understood his words.

"Oh. It might not be in stock?" She couldn't think about that. It had to be in stock.

"He'll call in the morning to see if anyone in town has it. Otherwise, he'll have to order it." Cole took a sip of his water.

She sat back, trying not to feel defeated. "And how long will that take?"

"Depends."

Shanna rubbed her temples. "I can't miss my parents' anniversary party."

"Let's see what happens in the morning." He reached over and grabbed the ketchup. "For now, let's finish our burgers."

After dinner, as they walked out of the diner, Ada called out, "Thanks for coming. Come back real soon."

Cole waved, then said to Shanna, "Do you need to get right back?"

She shrugged. "What do you have in mind?"

"A walk down Main." He inclined his head toward the street. "It might take your mind off your worries."

Shanna didn't normally take time in the evenings to do anything but work.

"Or we can go back to the inn," he offered.

She brightened. Maybe a walk would do her good. "I think I'd like to explore this town. A walk sounds great. I can work off some of that amazing dinner."

"Ada makes a delicious burger, that's for sure." He smiled and Shanna ignored the fluttering effect it had on her heart.

They started walking down the street. Though the stores were closed, light emanated from each of the windows creating an almost magical glow along the road. "Do you have a favorite restaurant in Denver?" he asked, breaking the silence.

"Hmmm. I don't think so." She rarely took the time to go to restaurants. Her go-to was home delivery.

"Haven't taken the time to find one?" he asked.

He was perceptive. "I tend to work a lot," she said.

Shanna stopped in front of a window where a vintage dress adorned a mannequin. "That's beautiful." A necklace displayed on the table caught her gaze. "My mom would love that." She stepped closer to get a better view.

Cole moved next to her. "The store will be open in the morning."

"I'd love to give her that for their anniversary. I didn't have a chance to get them gifts." She sounded like she was too busy to do anything. Maybe she was.

"What about your dad?" Cole asked.

Shanna peered through the window. She pointed at a silver pocket watch displayed next to a box. "I think he'd love that. He used to tell me a story about how his grandpa had a pocket watch." Memories of her dad's stories warmed her.

"Sounds like that's the gift for him." Cole nodded.

"They've been married for thirty years. That's a long time. These days, I can't even maintain a relationship for thirty days. Maybe not even thirty minutes." She laughed because she was kidding. Kind of.

"I bet that isn't true." He put his hands in his pockets.

They began walking again. "Oh, it is. Actually, I haven't had time for any kind of a relationship for a long time. I can't even remember the last time I went out." She hadn't seen anyone since she'd broken up with Greg.

"I don't find that hard to believe," he said while he gazed ahead.

She stopped. "You think I'm a workaholic, don't you?" If she was honest, he wasn't wrong. Her life did revolve around her job. But that wasn't a bad thing.

He shrugged.

"I'm driven," she said, defending herself. "It's good."

"Is it?" He left the question hanging.

They started walking along the street again past a gift shop and a candy store.

When someone opened a door up ahead, some country music filtered out. The closer they got, the louder it was.

"Ah, sounds like The Byrnes are playing." He moved his head in tempo to the music.

Shanna looked at him.

"A local band," he said. "They're pretty good." He tapped his leg like it was a drum.

Trying to show him that she could enjoy herself and do something spontaneous, she said, "Let's go listen to them."

"Really?" He peered at her with a surprised expression.

"Sure." The corners of her mouth tugged up. "See, I can do something besides work."

"After you, then," he said, gesturing for her to go inside the Moonlit Bar.

"I need to use the restroom. I'll meet you at a table?" she said.

Cole tipped his head.

COLE MADE his way over to see Joel and LeRoy, his buddies from high school. "Hey, guys. How're things?"

"Pretty good. Who's that woman you're with? I don't recognize her," LeRoy said, then adjusted his black cowboy hat.

Cole sat on the stool next to Joel. "Her car broke down about ten miles out of town, so I towed it to the garage."

Joel slugged him in the arm. "Well, aren't you the lucky one?"

Shaking his head, Cole said, "I'm only showing her around town because her car won't be fixed until tomorrow. Nothing else."

"Such a gentleman," LeRoy said. Both he and Joel started chuckling.

"Oh, hi, Cole." He turned to see Laurel dressed in a white skirt, a red shirt, and cowboy boots. She placed her arms around his neck. "Come dance with me."

"Thanks, but I can't." He removed her arms from around him and stood.

She leaned into him, her floral perfume filling his nose. "Why not?" she asked.

"He's got a woman with him," Joel said, inclining his head toward the bathroom.

"You what?" Laurel frowned.

"It's not like that," Cole said, waving his hand.

Laurel perked up. "Then come dance with me." She wrapped her arms around his waist just as Shanna walked out of the bathroom. Cole stepped away from Laurel.

Shanna made her way over to the table. Before she could say anything, he asked, "Would you like to dance?"

"Uh, sure."

Ignoring Laurel's obvious displeasure, Cole held out his hand to lead Shanna to the dance floor. As soon as she put her hand in his, a current of energy zipped up his arm. He pulled her close and they started doing the two-step.

After a minute or so, he said, "You're good. You've done the two-step before?"

"No, but I'm a quick study," she said with a smile that made him happy her car broke down.

He twirled her around the room while they listened to, "It's Five O'Clock Somewhere." He hadn't gone dancing in quite a while and he was surprised at how natural it felt having Shanna in his arms.

When the song changed to Toby Keith's, "Should've Been a Cowboy," people moved to the center.

"Line dancing," he said, hoping she knew what that was.

"Okay." Shanna watched the people dancing, but she kept making the wrong turns and kicking the wrong foot.

Cole moved in closer to her. "Stay with me." He tried to show her the moves. Without warning, she kicked him in the shin.

She gasped, then covered her mouth. "Oh, no. I'm so sorry," she said when she removed her hand from her mouth.

"No worries." He winced but didn't want her to see him in pain, so he masked it. "I'm fine."

"I don't think I'm a very good line dancer," she said. "I guess I'm not a quick study, after all."

"It takes some practice." He wanted to reassure her that she could follow the steps. Mostly, he wanted to keep dancing with her.

She tried again, but this time she dissolved into giggles as she tried to keep up.

Cole watched her and couldn't help but laugh himself.

She gazed at him with an offended expression.

He lifted his hand and said, "I'm not laughing *at* you. I'm laughing *with* you."

"Sure you are." She put her hands on her hips and stopped.

LeRoy bumped right into her and knocked her to the ground.

Cole rushed to her and extended his hand. "I'm so sorry." He pulled her to her feet.

"It wasn't your fault," she said.

"I'm sorry that my friend, LeRoy is such a buffoon when it comes to dancing." Why couldn't LeRoy watch where he was going?

"Sorry about that. Didn't see ya," LeRoy said. "And I am not a buffoon." He did a ridiculous dance move.

Shanna rubbed her hip, then smiled.

"Maybe we should go back to walking outside," Cole said, feeling bad that she'd been knocked down.

"I think I'll go sit this one out," Shanna said.

Before Cole could say anything, Laurel was in front of him. "Come on, Cole. Dance with me."

"You should go dance with her," Shanna said. "She probably won't end up on the floor."

"Please?" Laurel said.

Cole didn't want to dance with Laurel but decided he'd give her this dance, hoping she'd leave him alone afterward.

SITTING ON A BARSTOOL, Shanna watched Cole dance with the brown-haired woman with large hoop earrings, bright red lipstick, and a white skirt that was way too short. Then there were the cowboy boots. Who wore those with a micro-mini skirt?

A twinge of something passed through Shanna, but she shrugged it off. She didn't care if this woman was dancing close to Cole. He was free to dance with whomever he pleased. It didn't matter to Shanna, and it didn't bother her in the least to see them in each other's arms as they partnered around the room. Why would it bother her? She'd barely met the man.

"Can I get you a drink? Make up for knocking ya to the ground?" LeRoy said, pushing his black cowboy hat back.

"Oh, no thanks." She didn't need a drink. She needed to get on her way. The sooner she could get back to the inn, the sooner she could go back over her presentation, go to sleep, and then wake up with her car fixed and ready to go. She didn't want to waste time with small talk.

"I feel bad I knocked ya over." LeRoy sat next to her, holding a drink.

"It's fine." She waved her hand. "I should have gotten out of your way." She was trying to think of a polite way to exit.

"Where ya from?" He sipped his drink.

"I live in Denver, but I'm on my way to Amarillo, where I grew up." She glanced around the bar looking for an escape.

"And your car broke down?"

She nodded.

"Jimmy Bob will have ya up and runnin' in no time. Cole used to be a real good mechanic until he up and left town to be a big ol' lawyer," he said, then took a swig.

Though she wanted to leave, she found herself interested in what LeRoy had to say about Cole. "Oh, yeah?"

"It was right after Deidre broke off their engagement. She ran off with some guy she'd been seeing on the side. Made ol' Cole pretty sad," LeRoy said.

"I didn't know." She glanced over at Cole. "He was engaged?"

"Uh, huh. He left town and next thing we know, he's in some law firm up north and has some new girlfriend. Then, just as quick, he left all that to come help after his dad passed." He jutted his chin toward where Cole was. "Glad he's back now. Hopin' he stays."

No longer in a hurry to leave. Shanna asked, "You've been friends a long time?"

"Since we was kids. Used to ride fences together and get into all sorts of trouble." He chuckled. "But that's all behind us now." He paused, "Well, most of it." He laughed again.

She didn't want to seem too interested, but, despite herself, she wanted to know about that woman on the dance floor. Was she someone Cole had been involved with? "And the woman dancing with him?"

LeRoy removed his hat and ran his fingers through his longish, straight dark hair. "Oh, that's just Laurel. She's been hittin' on him ever since he got back." He put his hat back on.

"I see." Somehow, that made Shanna feel better. Kind of. In a way that didn't matter to her because she didn't care who Cole danced with.

LeRoy leaned in and whispered, "No competition for ya, though."

"Competition?" She looked at him incredulously, then laughed. "I hardly know him. There's nothing between us."

LeRoy gave her a look, then said, "Uh, huh."

"Seriously. I'm only here one night until my car is fixed. He's been kind enough to show me around. That's all there is to it." And that was the truth. He was a nice guy she'd completely forget about in a few days.

LeRoy nodded, then smirked. "Whatever ya say."

Cole returned with Laurel trailing behind him.

"Thanks, Cole. That was such a fun dance. We should do it again." She sidled up closer to him. Shanna rolled her eyes. *This woman is so obvious.*

He stepped closer to Shanna. "I'm going to take Shanna back to the inn. Maybe another time."

Laurel's smile faded. She gave Shanna the once over. "Okay. I guess."

Cole motioned for Shanna to head toward the door and Shanna was more than happy to jump off the barstool and leave the bar. And Laurel.

Outside, the cool, late spring air felt refreshing after being in the bar that kept getting stuffier by the moment.

"Seems like this is quite the hangout," Shanna said.

"I don't come here much." Cole plunged his hands into the pockets of his jeans as they walked.

"You're a homebody?" She studied him.

He shrugged. "I did all that when I was younger. I guess it's not how I want to spend my time anymore."

Trying to fish for information, even though she reassured herself she didn't care, she said, "I appreciate you showing me around, but I think it made Laurel a little jealous."

Cole shook his head. "You know, I keep telling her I'm not interested."

"She seems quite persistent." It was obvious to anyone with eyes that Laurel was after Cole.

"That's a good word for it." He glanced up at the sky.

"So, you're not interested in Laurel or just not interested in dating?" Shanna was only trying to make small talk as they walked down Main Street.

"Hmm." He kicked a rock off the sidewalk. "Both, I think."

"Why?" She wanted to know more about Cole. For some reason, as they talked, she felt so comfortable with him. It was like they'd known each other for years.

He glanced at her. "That's a long story."

Shanna gave a nod. He obviously didn't want to talk about his past. She wasn't going to push him because he was entitled to his privacy.

When they got to the inn, Cole said, "I hope you enjoyed a little bit of the town."

"I did." Juniper Springs wasn't too bad of a place. It wasn't where she'd want to live, but she could see its charm for other people.

"Would you like anything?" Cole asked as they walked in the door.

"Thanks, but I need to work on my presentation. Hopefully, I can get on the internet in my room." There were some final touches she wanted to add specifically to the Instagram plan.

"Good luck with that." He smiled, making Shanna's pulse quicken.

"Thanks," she said, part of her wanting to drag out the goodbye.

"Good night." He tipped his hat to her, and she ascended the stairs.

Inside her room, she refused to let herself think about Cole or how good it felt to be in his arms while they danced. She refused to let herself think about how relaxed she felt with him. Or what it might be like to spend more time with him.

Instead, she went directly to her computer and fired it up, determined to spend time working on the Instagram campaign she'd designed.

CHAPTER 5

*S*hanna awoke early in the morning, the scent of bacon and fresh-brewed coffee wafting through her room, which made her stomach rumble.

She reminded herself that she wanted to be at the garage first thing so she could find out about her car. She slipped into a light blue dress and took a little extra time to brush her long hair and apply some light make up for no other reason except she would be seeing her parents today.

Descending the stairs, she saw Cole at the front desk wearing jeans and a grey t-shirt that showed off his defined biceps. Her heart pinged in her chest. *Stop that. He's a nice guy, but that's all there is to it. Nothing more.*

Cole looked up at her and a smile edged across his lips. "Good morning."

"Hi." She smoothed her hair, hating that she found his smile so appealing.

"You look nice," he said. His dark brown hair fell across his forehead, drawing attention to his ruggedly handsome face.

"Thank you." Warmth crept up her neck.

He stood and crossed the lobby to her. "We have breakfast in the dining room. Fresh baked biscuits and gravy, fruit, eggs, and, of course, bacon. Because what is breakfast without bacon? We also have some orange juice and coffee."

She tried not to notice how his cobalt blue eyes sparkled. "Sounds delicious," she said.

Belle walked in. "Oh, good morning, Shanna. You look lovely." Belle's voice was full of warmth.

"Thank you." She placed her hair behind her ears.

"Come in and eat. There's plenty of food. I made the biscuits myself. It's Cole's favorite," she said, her eyes filled with kindness. "Cole, come on in and have some breakfast. I'll man the desk."

Shanna laughed to herself. Belle was quite obvious in her attempt to put the two of them together. Maybe, and this was a big maybe, *if* they didn't live in different places and *if* she even had time to consider dating, Cole would be someone she might date. But as it was, Belle's attempts would be in vain.

"I was going to—" Cole started.

"Nonsense. You need a good breakfast," Belle said, motioning to the dining room.

Cole smiled in a way that seemed to indicate that even though he was a grown man, he knew he'd have to listen to his mom. Their relationship was sweet.

"I suppose we should sit together, or my mom might make a scene," Cole said with a tilt of his head.

Shanna bit back a smile. "I don't mind."

Cole led her over to the table where the food sat. "You really should try the biscuits," he said, pointing at the white, fluffy bread.

"Oh, I will." She intended to try everything.

Cole laughed.

"What?" She gazed at him, not sure what she'd said that was funny.

"Most women I know would only eat the fruit."

"I love fruit, too. But fresh baked biscuits? I'm definitely eating those." Shanna loaded her white porcelain plate. If things worked out right, she'd be leaving soon and probably wouldn't eat again until she got to Amarillo, so she wanted to eat plenty.

46

"I'd say you've surprised me," Cole said. He held a plate with biscuits and gravy and several pieces of bacon.

"Really?" She liked that she surprised him.

"A hamburger last night and now biscuits and gravy. I like it when a woman eats real food." He grabbed some silverware and napkins.

They sat at a small round table with a pale-yellow tablecloth near the window.

"I guess I like to eat." She shrugged, then bit into the light, flaky biscuit. "Mmm, this is so good." She wasn't used to homemade meals since her cooking skills were pretty much nil.

"The sausage my mom used in the gravy is from Curly." He bit into a slice of bacon. "And so is this."

"A friend of yours?" The people in Juniper Springs had names she didn't encounter much in Denver.

"No." He shook his head.

She gazed at him and pulled her eyebrows together. "Huh?"

"One of our pigs." He took a bite of his biscuits and gravy.

Shanna blinked a couple of times. *Curly?* "I'm eating your pet pig?" She didn't think she'd be able to eat another bite.

"No." He held his hand up. "Not a pet."

"But you named him." How could she possibly eat a pig named Curly? She wasn't sure she'd ever be able to eat pork again in any form.

As if it were no big deal, Cole said, "I name all of them. Makes it easier to keep track." He took another bite.

She felt guilty thinking of a cute little pig named Curly running around in the grass simply wanting to enjoy his life. It reminded her of *Charlotte's Web*, which she'd read as a girl.

As if sensing her discomfort, Cole said, "Curly lived a great life. He had plenty to eat, got lots of exercise, and we took good care of him."

Shanna had never thought much about the food she ate. She wasn't sure how she felt, except that it was an obvious example of how different her life was from Cole's.

"We have a dog named Ginger," he said. "We mainly raise beef

47

cattle, but we also have chickens, some pigs, and a milk goat named Lois." Cole sat back.

"Lois?" Shanna imagined that to be a perfect name for a milk goat —if one were going to name a milk goat. "The only animal I've had was Taffy, my cat."

"Most of us here raised animals from the time we were young. We were all involved in 4-H doing different projects. My mom was our leader. She still teaches sewing and woodworking to the 4-H kids."

"Your mom does woodworking?" Shanna wasn't sure she could visualize Belle using power tools and making things out of wood. Her mom would never do anything like that.

"She's made some amazing pieces." He pointed to a chair across the room. "Like that one."

Shanna gazed at the light wood chair with curved arms and a carved back. "Wow. That's beautiful." It was hard to believe anyone made a chair by hand. "Did you do woodworking?"

Cole shook his head. "I stuck to raising animals. I once sold a pig at the county fair for over six thousand dollars. And I sold a steer for fourteen thousand."

"Seriously? How?" Shanna couldn't believe someone would pay that much for an animal at some county fair in Nowhere, Colorado.

"All the kids in 4-H go to the county fair to show their projects and at the end, we have a big auction for the ones who raised animals. People come from all over the county to bid. It's how I paid my way through college. That and working at the garage fixing cars." Cole sat back.

"What made you decide to go into law?" Shanna was very interested to hear his answer."

He leaned in. "Long story."

"You seem to have long stories," she said with a twinge of disappointment.

"How's breakfast?" Belle said as she approached the table.

"I love the biscuits," Shanna said. "Cole pointed out that chair you made."

Belle waved her hand. "He always does that. I need to move that thing."

"Why? It's so beautiful." Shanna was still in awe that someone made a chair by hand.

"I don't want to draw attention," Belle said. "I just like making things out of wood. My dad taught me. We used to spend hours in his woodshop when I was a young girl, making things and talking about life. Ah, such good memories."

"Does he live here?" Shanna asked. She could only imagine the gorgeous things he'd made over the years.

"No, no. He passed some time ago. When Cole was in high school." Sadness flashed across her face. "Car accident out on the highway."

"I'm so sorry." Shanna's heart ached for Belle and Cole.

Belle gazed over at the chair. "Making things out of wood is my way of remembering him."

"Excuse me, do you have any almond milk?" a middle-aged woman with short black hair asked.

"Let me go check," Belle said. "I'll be back in a bit." She turned and left the table.

"Your mom is awesome," Shanna said. "She's so sincere and hospitable." Shanna almost felt like she belonged here. Except, she reminded herself, she didn't.

"I think she's pretty awesome myself. I was very lucky when it came to parents." Cole finished his orange juice.

Shanna's phone vibrated. It was her boss. "Hello?" she said as professionally as possible.

"I need you to make a couple of changes to the proposal for the Glasden Group," Renae said with the familiar you-don't-have-a-life-except-to-be-at-my-beck-and-call intonation.

"All right. Can you email them to me? I'm not at my computer." Shanna would make changes to the proposal and send them back to Renae to keep her happy and prove that Shanna deserved the senior position.

"Yes. But I want to see the new proposal this afternoon," she said in her customary demanding tone.

Shanna cleared her throat. "That shouldn't be a problem." Whatever else happened today, she'd need to get these changes done and sent back.

"I'll talk to you later then." Renae wasn't one for niceties. She was a driven woman, and an example of what ambition could do. Shanna wanted to emulate her. At least, she thought she did.

"Yes. Thank you. Bye." Shanna ended the call.

"Your boss?" Cole said with raised eyebrows.

"Yeah. She *actually* is a workaholic. She never takes time off." Shanna couldn't remember the last time Renae took a vacation.

"That must be hard for her family," Cole said.

"She doesn't have a family. Only her job at Rocky Mountain Public Relations." It kind of sounded hollow to Shanna—something she hadn't noticed before.

Cole's phone buzzed. He looked at the screen. "It's Jimmy Bob."

"I should've given him my number," Shanna said. She didn't want to make Cole be the go-between.

"You can talk to him." Cole answered the phone and handed it to Shanna.

"Hello?" she said.

There was a pause and then a slow, "Uhhhh."

"Jimmy Bob? This is Shanna. I have Cole's phone." she said, hoping to clear up his confusion.

"Ohhhh. Hi." She could imagine the expression on his face as recognition hit him. Jimmy Bob seemed to be a genuinely nice guy, like Cole.

"Do you have news about my car?" She hoped he'd say that he'd found the part and could have her back on the road in a few hours so she'd make it in time for most of the festivities for her parents. Although, if she were being completely honest, there was a part of her that wasn't anxious to leave Juniper Springs.

"I'm trying to find a water pump for you," he said cheerfully.

"Thank you," she said, waiting for him to say something else.

After a long pause, he said, "I just wanted you to know I'm working on it."

"I appreciate that." Shanna had hoped for better news. Or any news.

"If you give me your number I can call you directly," Jimmy Bob said.

Shanna gave him her phone number and then ended the call. She handed the phone back to Cole.

"Bad news?" Cole said with a sympathetic look in his eyes. Eyes that she could stare into for copious amounts of time.

"Oh, uh," she said. "Yeah, not really bad news or good news. He was calling to tell me he was looking for a water pump. Which I already knew." She wasn't sure of his purpose in calling since he didn't give her any new information.

Cole nodded. "Jimmy Bob likes to keep everyone updated. He's good like that."

Shanna let out a long breath. "I only hope it can be fixed today and I can get to the party. My mom will be so disappointed—"

"Let's not go there," Cole said, cutting her off. "Things will work out."

She admired Cole's optimism. Maybe he was right. She hoped everything would work out.

"After we finish breakfast, we can go to that shop on Main and get the gifts for your parents. Maybe by then Jimmy Bob will have more information."

"That's a good idea." Shanna appreciated that Cole was helping her, even if it made it difficult to remember that she'd likely never see him again.

They finished breakfast and stood.

"Oh, I'm sorry I didn't make it back," Belle said as she walked over to their table. "I was checking out the nicest couple from Oklahoma. They're on their way to a funeral, so I boxed up some food for them to take on the road."

"That was kind of you," Shanna said. Belle had to be one of the most thoughtful women she knew. She seemed to think of others so easily. Shanna rarely thought of others because she was so wrapped up in her projects at work.

Belle shrugged as if it was nothing.

"We're going shopping," Shanna said.

"You are?" Belle smirked as she cast a gaze at Cole. "Hmm."

"Shanna doesn't know her way around so I'm taking her over to the vintage shop on Main to pick up gifts for her parents," Cole said a bit defensively. Shanna assumed from his mom's reaction that he didn't shop much.

"I saw a necklace and a pocket watch through the window last night on our way to dancing," Shanna said, wanting to come to Cole's defense.

"You went *dancing*?" Belle said with raised eyebrows.

"If you need me, you can call," Cole said as he made his way to the door. He motioned for Shanna to follow.

"I won't need you. I can take care of things here. Take as long as you want," she said with a lilt to her voice.

"Thanks, Mom," Cole said over his shoulder.

Outside the front door of the inn, Shanna said, "Your mom seemed surprised you went dancing."

"I guess." He put on his cowboy hat and started walking along the sidewalk.

"Why?" she prodded, stepping up next to him.

"Not my thing." He shrugged a shoulder.

"You were very good for it not being your thing," she said, not letting it drop.

"I used to dance a lot, but that was a long time ago." The way he said it let Shanna know he didn't want to talk about it anymore.

Shanna didn't say anything else, but she guessed it had something to do with his broken engagement.

CHAPTER 6

The warm country air filtered through Shanna's hair while they walked along the street to Main. If she wasn't in such a rush to get to Amarillo, she might enjoy taking a few days to explore this picturesque town, a thought that surprised her.

Cole opened the door to the vintage shop, Yesteryear's Gifts, and Shanna walked in. Inside, she was drawn to a cream-colored dress with intricate lace and some beading on the bodice.

"That is over eighty years old," said a short woman with her red hair twisted up and secured with a clip.

"The lace is so delicate." Shanna reached out and softly touched the elegant dress.

"It's a one-of-a-kind. Are you looking for a wedding dress?" she asked, then glanced between Cole and her.

"Oh, no. We aren't . . . I mean, I'm not . . . I thought it was a beautiful dress. That's all." Shanna tripped all over her words.

"I was going to say how surprised I'd be that Cole here would have a fiancée," the middle-aged woman said as she walked around Shanna.

Cole said, "Eleanor, this is Shanna. She's here until Jimmy Bob fixes her car."

Eleanor laid her hand across her chest. "Oh, I see."

Feeling like she needed to explain the situation, Shanna said, "My car broke down last night and Cole was nice enough to come and tow it into town."

"Cole is a pretty nice guy," Eleanor said, the corners of her mouth turned up.

Shanna smiled. That sentiment seemed to be the consensus in this town.

"Are you looking for anything in particular?" Eleanor asked.

"I'd love to look at that necklace." Shanna pointed to the one by the front window.

"And she was interested in the pocket watch, too," Cole added.

"We were window shopping last night and I saw the necklace and the watch." Shanna walked over to where the necklace was displayed. "I'm on my way to my parents' anniversary party and I didn't have a chance to get them their gifts yet." She was grateful she had an opportunity now to find something here, so she didn't have to go back to Amarillo empty handed and have to find them gifts there.

Eleanor handed Shanna the necklace. It was a golden locket with a speck of a diamond on the front and an etching. She opened the locket. "I could put in a picture of my brother and me when we were babies. My mom would love that," Shanna said.

"That'd be a very thoughtful gift." Eleanor smiled.

Shanna held it up and examined it even more closely. She should've gotten gifts earlier, but part of her was glad she'd waited because she would never have found something like this.

"And here's the pocket watch." Eleanor handed her the watch.

Shanna looked it over. "I love all the details on this. And it works?"

"Yes. And the chain is sterling silver," Eleanor said, pointing to it.

"I'll take both," Shanna said. It was an easy decision. Her parents had more than enough money to buy whatever they wanted, but neither had a gift like one of these. Shanna wanted to give them both something special.

"I'll wrap them up for you," Eleanor said. She walked to the back of the store.

Shanna made her way over to a display of hats. She picked up a burgundy one with a large flower on the side and put it on her head. "What do you think of this?" she said as she turned toward Cole.

"Looks great," Cole said.

"I wish we still wore hats like this." She gazed at herself in a gold leaf mirror hanging on the wall. "They're so bougie."

"*Bougie?*" Cole said, his eyebrows pulled together.

"Yes, you know, bougie." She thought for a moment. "Fancy or luxurious."

Cole nodded with a look of confusion on his face. Shanna found a brown man's hat and handed it to him.

He set the brown hat on his head.

"You look so dapper," she said, adjusting his hat and trying not to react to their close proximity. Their gazes caught, and, for a moment, they both stood there transfixed.

Cole broke the spell. He tugged her over to the mirror where they admired themselves, then pulled several different faces before dissolving into laughter.

"We should all wear hats like this," Shanna said, enjoying Cole's playful attitude.

Shanna pulled out her phone and snapped a selfie with Cole, noting that although she enjoyed him in this hat, she much preferred his cowboy hat he held in his hand.

"Here you are," Eleanor said as she returned to the front of the store. "I've wrapped them both in our special paper," she said with a cheerful tone as she handed Shanna the package.

Shanna removed her hat. "Thank you so much. My parents will love these gifts."

Cole took off his hat. "Anything else you'd like to look at?"

Shanna gazed around the store. "I think I could spend a long time in here, but I need to get over to the garage so I can find out about my car." She had to focus on getting to Amarillo and then finding time to work on her presentation, she reminded herself. Being with Cole seemed to make her forget what she was doing.

Shanna paid for the gifts and placed them both in her bag.

They walked down Main and crossed the street so they could walk over to the garage.

"Hey, Jimmy Bob," Cole said as they entered the repair area.

Jimmy Bob was leaning over the front of a red truck. "Hey." He straightened. He had a smudge of grease on his cheek.

"Any news on the water pump?" Shanna asked eagerly.

"I've been calling my regular distributors, but none of 'em have one in stock for your Honda." He wiped at his face and left another smudge.

"What does that mean?" Shanna said, trying to ignore the grease marks.

"The best I can do, I think, is have one delivered from Denver." Jimmy Bob picked up a wrench from his toolbox.

"Today?" *Please say today.* If it wasn't today, she didn't know what she'd do.

Jimmy Bob scratched his head. "No. Sorry. It wouldn't be til Monday."

"*Monday?* I can't wait here until Monday. I need to get to Amarillo." Her voice hit a high pitch and she fisted her hands.

Jimmy Bob shrugged and gave her a sympathetic look.

Shanna's face warmed. She pushed out a breath. "There's no way to get it fixed today? No way at all?" There had to be something he could do.

Jimmy Bob shook his head. "I'm sorry. I tried real hard to find you a pump today. Real hard."

She rubbed her forehead. "It's not your fault. I know that. I'm just upset."

"I wish I could do more," Jimmy Bob said.

Weighing her options, Shanna said, "I'll get a rental car, I guess." That was the best solution she had. She'd drive the rental car to Amarillo, then return to Juniper Springs and get her car to drive back to Denver.

Jimmy Bob glanced at Cole, then back to Shanna. "Uh, we don't have rental cars here."

"What? You don't have a rental car agency in town?" She blinked back her disbelief.

"No, we don't," Jimmy Bob said in an apologetic tone.

"All right. Fine." She could feel her blood pressure rising. "Then I can take a bus."

Jimmy Bob made an I-hate-to-tell-you-this face. "No bus station, neither."

"Are you kidding me? No car rentals. No bus." What kind of town was this? She paced back and forth. "What about an Uber? Can I hire an Uber?"

"A what?" Jimmy Bob said, with a crinkled nose.

Shanna shook her head, her eyes burning. Missing her parents' party wasn't an option. She had to figure out a way to get to Amarillo from Juniper Springs, which had to be the smallest town she'd ever seen.

"We can figure out something," Cole said, holding his hands out.

"What? I have no car, no rentals, no bus. Is there an airport?" She chortled because she already knew the answer.

"Maybe someone is going that way and can give you a lift?" Jimmy Bob offered.

"I guess I could go out on the highway and hitchhike," she said facetiously, but it was lost on Jimmy Bob.

"I'll take you," Cole said.

"What?" She turned and stared at him, not sure she'd heard him correctly.

"I'll drive you to Amarillo," he said as if it was the obvious solution.

Shanna blinked, then looked at him. "I can't ask you to do that."

"I haven't been to Amarillo, and I'd like to see it." He shrugged like it was no big deal at all to drive her all that way.

Shanna studied him. Was he actually this nice? He'd drive her all the way to Amarillo? "It's almost a four-hour drive from here, I think. That's a long way."

"I don't mind." He seemed to be serious.

Waving her hand, she said, "I'm sure you have better things to do than drive to Amarillo today. Plus, your mom needs you." Shanna couldn't impose on him like this, even if it was the only way she'd be there in time for the celebration.

"Look." He held a hand out in front of him. "You're stranded here. Your parents are having a big event that's important to you."

Shanna couldn't argue with him because he was right.

"Unless I drive you," he stepped closer to her, "you'll miss it."

Shanna's phone buzzed. Hesitantly, she answered it. "Hi, Mom."

"Are you almost here?" Her mom's voice was full of excitement and Shanna hesitated to tell her she was stuck in some small town with no way to get home.

"Uh." Shanna didn't know what to say.

"Shanna?" her mom said.

She drew in a deep breath of courage. "You see, Mom, I'm not exactly . . ."

"What are you trying to say?" In her mind, she could see the look on her mom's face.

"Well, my car broke down." There, it was out.

"It broke down? Where?" Her mom sounded worried.

"I called Daddy last night because it was making a strange noise. I guess he didn't tell you. Apparently, my car needs a water pump, and we can't get one here until Monday." She gritted her teeth waiting for her mom's reaction.

"Oh, dear. What does that mean? You're still coming to our celebration? You have to be here." Her mom's voice seemed to rise an octave with every sentence.

"I'm trying to figure something out, I promise." She wasn't going to add that there was no possibility of renting a car or taking a bus or hiring an Uber.

"Your father can come and get you," her mom said.

"No, no. I don't want him to do that. You need him there for the brunch and the celebration. This is your anniversary." It wouldn't be much of a celebration for her mom if her dad was on the road to Juniper Springs.

"All right, I can send your brother."

"No, Mom. I don't want Patrick to miss any of the events either.

Besides, Lacey will need his help with everything there." Shanna twisted her hair around her finger.

"Well, we absolutely need you here so—"

"Mom, wait." She gazed at Cole. He had offered. Could she take him up on it? Would it be too much of an imposition? "I think . . . I *may* have a ride."

Cole nodded.

"You do? With whom?" Her mom sounded surprised.

"The guy who towed my car." It sounded a little absurd.

"Do you know anything about him?" her mom said, concern evident in her tone.

"I know enough." She couldn't possibly explain to her mom what a kind and generous person Cole was and how she felt safe and secure when she was around him, because she didn't quite understand it herself.

"Are you sure he isn't an ax murderer or something?" her mom said, completely serious.

"I don't think he's going to do anything sinister to me." She made a cringey face at Cole, who simply smiled.

"I'm going to worry until I see you."

"Please, don't." She didn't want her mom to fret about Cole, because she wasn't the least bit concerned about driving with him. In fact, if she were being honest, she was looking forward to it. "I'll be fine. But I won't be there in time for the brunch. I'm so sorry."

"Don't worry about that. As long as you'll be here today, and especially for the dinner and dance tonight. I don't want you to miss that."

"I won't." She wanted to reassure her mom she was going to try as hard as she could to come for at least part of the celebration.

"I'll see you today then?" Her mom seemed placated.

"Yes, you will."

After Shanna ended the call, she said to Cole, "Are you sure about this?"

"Yes, ma'am." He dipped his head and a lock of his hair fell across his forehead.

"Can I make a request?" she asked, then bit her lip.

"Sure."

"Please, stop calling me ma'am. It makes me feel super old."

Cole laughed. "I'll try."

"You surely aren't old," Jimmy Bob said. "You're a decent lookin' young woman." He grinned and it made Shanna giggle.

She turned to Cole. "I guess we need to go back to the inn so I can get my things." She was grateful that Cole's offer to drive her had solved her problem. She was even more grateful that it would allow them to spend more time together. Despite their obvious differences and everything else stacked against them, she didn't want her time with Cole to end quite yet.

"I'll keep in touch with you about your car," Jimmy Bob said. "If we can get the water pump early enough on Monday, I'll have you back on the road by the early afternoon."

Monday. A sinking feeling washed over her. "I have a big presentation on Tuesday that I absolutely can't miss. I've been working on it like crazy. It's a big account. You know, my chance to shine, maybe get a promotion, and all that. So the car absolutely has to be done on Monday." She couldn't emphasize that enough.

"I'll do my best," Jimmy Bob said with a confident nod.

Cole started walking toward the doorway. "Let's get your stuff. I need to take care of a couple of things and get my truck ready."

"The tow truck?" she said with a smirk.

He quirked his eyebrow. "If you'd like to arrive in style, I can arrange to take it."

"I think your Ford truck will be fine." She turned to Jimmy Bob. "Thank you for taking care of my car. I appreciate it."

"Sure thing, Miss Shanna," Jimmy Bob said.

They walked back to the inn and Shanna went up to her room.

"Mom?" Cole said as he entered the kitchen, the smell of homemade bread floating on the air.

His mom looked up from the counter where she was cooling the fresh-baked loaves. "Did you take Shanna to the vintage shop?"

"Yeah, she found some gifts for her parents." Cole reached for a loaf.

His mom slapped at his hand. "Now, now. Let these cool."

"You know I can't resist your bread," he said with a smile.

"I'm glad Shanna found some gifts. She's a sweet, thoughtful girl. And beautiful to boot." She eyed him. "She'd make a lovely companion for someone."

It didn't take a rocket scientist to understand his mom's implication. He hesitated to tell her he was going to take Shanna to Amarillo for fear of her reading more into it than there was, but she had to know he'd be gone. "Mom," he said. "I'm going to drive to Amarillo."

Her head snapped up and she tried to hide her grin. "You are, are you?"

Trying to put it all in perspective for his mom, he said, "Yeah. If I don't take her to her parents' party, she'll have to miss it, which would disappoint her family." That sounded benign. Because it was. He was simply driving a stranded motorist to an event. No one had to make anything more out of it.

She leaned against the counter and with a tilted head said, "So you just happened to volunteer?"

"I thought it was the polite thing to do." He walked over to the sink and took out a glass from the cupboard. He needed a drink of water because his throat was suddenly dry.

"Of course, it is. The polite thing to do," she said, nodding.

He filled his glass with water and took a long swig. "But that means I won't be here, obviously."

His mom stepped over to him and placed her hand on his shoulder. "Son, I'll be fine. You take our guest *politely* to Amarillo and I'll take care of everything here."

Madi burst into the kitchen and glanced between Cole and his mom. "What's going on?"

"Cole will be going to Amarillo today." His mom set the large mixing bowl in the sink.

"How come?" Madi opened the refrigerator and grabbed a carrot.

"Because someone needs a ride there." Cole's mom said it as if she were singing, which made Cole roll his eyes.

"Ah, it wouldn't be that guest with the blond hair and big blue eyes, would it?" Madi giggled.

"It is," his mom said, putting one hand on her hip.

"Awesome." Madi bobbed her head. "You haven't dated anyone since . . ."

"We are not *dating*. I literally met her yesterday. And I only offered to take her to Amarillo, because otherwise she'll miss an important event." His mom and cousin were being ridiculous.

"So you're just being a nice guy?" Madi said with mock seriousness.

"Yeah." He emphasized his response.

"That's all?" Madi took a bite of her carrot.

"Yes." That was all. Why did these two women find that so hard to believe?

"And the fact that she's beautiful has nothing to do with it?" Madi said.

"No." Wait. Did he mean no? Or did he mean yes? Madi was trying to trip him up.

"You admit she's beautiful?" Madi said, then glanced over at her aunt.

Cole narrowed his eyes at his cousin. "I'm done with this conversation," he said over his shoulder as he left the kitchen.

"I know I'm convinced," Madi called after him.

Cole shook his head. Both his mom and Madi were romanticizing this whole thing. He was simply helping out another person. That was all. It didn't matter that he thought she was beautiful. Or that he enjoyed talking to her. Or that her eyes lit up when she smiled. He wasn't taking her to Amarillo to date her. Period.

CHAPTER 7

*S*hanna grabbed her bags and headed down the stairs. She was grateful Cole was driving her to Amarillo so she wouldn't miss the celebration, especially since there didn't seem to be any other options, but that warning bell was sounding in her ears. Was this the wrong thing to do?

"Hi," Belle said, breaking Shanna out of her thoughts.

"Oh, hi. I guess I'm checking out." She set her bag next to the desk.

"I heard that Cole is going to take you to Amarillo." Belle placed the guest book in front of Shanna and handed her a pen.

"He is. I'm very thankful." She signed the book and gave Belle her credit card.

"He's always been helpful and kind to others." Belle ran the credit card and gave it back to Shanna.

"I can see that. I feel bad making him drive me so far." She did feel bad. Mostly.

"He's young and he likes to drive his big, black truck."

"Thank you for letting him take me. I know you need him here." Shanna hoped it didn't cause any problems for Cole to leave. As strange as it sounded, she'd come to care about Belle and didn't want to leave her in a lurch.

Belle waved her hand. "Don't even trouble your mind about it. I'll get along fine. I have Madison to help me."

"He should be able to make it back late tonight." Shanna didn't want to take Cole from his duties in Juniper Springs any longer than she needed to.

Belle gave an amiable smile. "He doesn't need to rush back here. Madison and I have everything under control. He can take as long as he needs."

Shanna studied Belle because there seemed to be an undertone to her words. Changing the subject, she said, "What is that heavenly smell?"

"I baked some bread." Belle reached over to the counter and grabbed a wrapped loaf. "For your trip." She grabbed another loaf. "For your parents. Please wish them a happy anniversary."

"That is so thoughtful of you. Thank you." Shanna held the still-warm loaves emanating the fresh-baked scent. She didn't think her mom had ever had homemade bread.

"Cole will come in and get your bags and take them to his truck," Belle said.

Shanna nodded. She wanted to hug Belle, but her hands were full. "Thank you again for a wonderful stay. The room was beautiful, and the bed was so comfortable. The food was amazing. I'd give it six stars out of five," she said with exuberance.

"I hope you'll come back again real soon." The way she said it left no doubt she wanted to see Shanna again.

Cole walked in the door wearing his cowboy hat and boots, making Shanna's heart somersault. She shook out the thoughts that tried to settle in her brain. "I'll get your bags for you," he said.

"Thank you," Shanna said.

"Drive safe." Belle gave them a wave.

They walked out the front door and over to Cole's black truck.

"I really do appreciate this. I know it's a long drive and I intend to pay you not only for the gas but also for taking the time to drive me there." Shanna didn't want Cole to think she was taking advantage of his kindness.

He shook his head. "I don't need your money." Cole set her bags on the back seat in the cab.

"I know you don't, but it'd make me feel better." Somehow, giving him money might make it easier for her to keep this less personal—something she was struggling to do.

Cole shut the back door to the cab. He peered at her and said, "In exchange for payment, how about you help someone in the future?"

That wasn't what she expected him to say. "Uh, I guess I could do that." She'd probably have to set a reminder on her phone to look for someone to help because it wasn't a natural tendency for her like it seemed to be for Cole.

"Then we're all settled." He smiled and Shanna was almost positive the sun glinted off his teeth.

Cole opened the passenger door and Shanna slid into the leather seat. She shut the door, then inhaled the woodsy scent mixed with spearmint, finding it even more difficult to control her racing thoughts.

Cole opened his door and got inside the truck. He started the engine, which roared to life.

"Is this an eight-cylinder?"

"Yes, ma . . . I mean, Shanna." He gave her a nod.

"Thank you for not calling me ma'am and making me feel old." Her mom was a ma'am—she wasn't.

"It's a habit, but I'll do my best," he said.

They pulled out onto the highway and Shanna sat back, her muscles relaxing against the seat.

"What kind of music do you prefer to listen to?" Cole asked.

"I usually listen to Taylor Swift." She loved Taylor's newest album.

"Of course," he said with a smile.

"What does that mean?" She gave him an expression of feigned indignation.

He glanced at her, then looked straight ahead through the windshield. "Women seem to love her music."

"You don't?"

He shrugged. "I'm more of a Zac Brown Band kind of a guy."

"Taylor speaks a lot of truth." More than one of Taylor's songs had touched her over the years.

"Does she?" Cole asked. "I admit, I don't listen to her music."

"She's been hurt by men, especially Greg, I mean, Jake Gyllenhaal." Thoughts of her first love, who'd trampled her heart, circled round her brain.

He gave her a sideways glance. "I've heard that. But it goes both ways," he said, fanning his hand out to his side.

"Sounds like there's a story there." Shanna was more than a little interested in hearing this story.

"It's a—"

"Long story. I know," she said with a laugh. "But guess what? We have a long drive and I'm a great listener." She wanted him to feel comfortable sharing his story with her.

Cole nodded and looked as if he were considering her words.

"Seriously. I am." She turned in her seat and watched him.

After a few moments, he said, "I was dating a woman for a couple of years, someone I'd known for a long time, and I finally got up the courage to ask her to marry me." He glanced out the side window.

Shanna kept her gaze on him.

"We were engaged for a few months. Started planning the wedding." He worked his jaw.

Shanna didn't say anything.

"One day, I came home from work and found a note in the kitchen." He tapped the steering wheel.

Shanna tensed while she waited for him to finish.

"She said she'd met someone else. She was sorry but she couldn't marry me. They ran off together somewhere." He adjusted his weight in his seat.

"A note?" She cringed at the thought.

"Yeah. A Note." He nodded and kept his gaze ahead.

"Not even face to face?" She couldn't imagine not having a conversation like that in person.

"Nope."

"I'm sorry. That's pretty callous." Her heart ached for the hurt that had caused him.

He let out a long breath. "Soured me on dating for a long time."

"I can understand why." She hadn't suffered a broken engagement per se, but she'd planned to marry Greg.

Silence hung over them for several miles. "Then, I finally decided it was time to meet someone else and get on with my life," he said.

"Oh?" This wasn't exactly what Shanna wanted to hear. Was he going to tell her he had a girlfriend back in Fort Collins?

"A woman I met after I started practicing law. Melissa." He reached up and massaged the back of his neck. "I thought I needed to give the whole love thing another shot, and it had been some years since Deidre had run off on me."

"What happened?" She was anxious to know.

"Things seemed to be progressing. We'd been together for almost a year and then I found out she was cheating on me with her ex. Almost the whole time."

Shanna covered her mouth. *Poor Cole.*

"Obviously, we broke up." He removed his hat and placed it next to him, then ran his fingers through his hair.

Cole had suffered some serious heartache and it made Shanna want to pull him into an embrace.

"It's the whole fool me once, fool me twice thing. I haven't dated anyone since Melissa."

Shanna could understand why Cole would be hesitant to trust any woman after his experiences. "I'm really sorry." She appreciated that he shared this with her. A part of her was relieved he wasn't attached to a woman, but the other part realized he had trust issues when it came to dating. She couldn't blame him. It was a good thing they weren't romantically involved. Right?

He shrugged. "It's in the past now."

"You've had it pretty rough with losing your dad, too."

Cole put his hat back on. "Yeah."

"You were close to him?"

He smiled and Shanna surmised he was thinking of happy memories. "Spent a lot of time doing chores with him, talking about every-thing under the sun while we rode horses, working with the cattle, and fixing a lot of fences."

Shanna tried to stop the images of Cole flexing his muscles as he worked around their ranch from dancing across her mind. It proved to be difficult.

"The inn, the garage, and the ranch are too much for my mom to handle by herself. Madi came to help, but the two of them need more help," he said with conviction. Shanna didn't have to wonder for a moment how he felt about his family and their businesses.

"What about your law career?" Shanna hoped she'd never have to give up her career, but meeting Belle made her understand why Cole wanted to help her.

"I still do some remote work, but I'm thinking about opening a practice in Juniper Springs." He adjusted his grip on the steering wheel.

"Really?" For a tiny moment, she'd thought if he went back to Fort Collins, which was about an hour from Denver, maybe, just maybe, they could see each other again. But if he moved permanently to Juniper Springs there was no chance for them. . . to what? She laughed to herself. Why was she even entertaining thoughts of seeing him after this weekend?

"I haven't decided quite what to do. I still have my apartment and I need to figure that all out," he said, jolting her out of her thoughts.

Shanna nodded.

After several minutes of silence, Cole glanced over at her and said," So now that I've shared my life story, how about you?"

She leaned her head against the window. "Not much to tell. You already know I grew up in Amarillo and moved to Denver to work in a public relations firm." That about summed up her life.

"Yeah, you told me that," he said. "What about your. . . personal life?"

She peered at him. "You mean, do I have a boyfriend?" She assumed that's what he was asking.

He adjusted his hat.

Since they still had miles to go, she figured she might as well share her love life aka love disaster. "We were high school sweethearts. The couple most likely to get married after graduation." She made a grand gesture with her hands. "When it came time for college, we attended different schools, but we decided to stay together. We, or maybe I, thought we had a future together."

"How did that work out?" Cole asked in a sincere tone.

Shanna stared down at her hands in her lap. "Long-distance relationships are hard. I wouldn't recommend ever doing one." She laughed softly. "But we managed to do it." She looked out the windshield, memories floating around her mind.

"And you got married?"

She shook her head. "No." Letting out a breath, she continued, "He accepted a position in Dallas and wanted me to move there, but I didn't want to go because I received a job offer in Denver. We tried to keep the relationship going but we finally broke up."

"I'm sorry." His voice was full of sympathy.

"I haven't seen him for a long time, but I hear from my mom, who is friends with his mom, that he's doing well and I'm happy for him." She meant it. She didn't have any ill will toward Greg. She had hoped they'd get married, but that isn't how it worked out. It was probably for the best.

He glanced at her. "And since then?"

"Since then? Hmmm. I guess my career has been my boyfriend." She recognized how pathetic that sounded. "Let's talk about something else."

CHAPTER 8

S hanna and Cole spent the next hour or so talking about music, movies, and their mutual dislike of politics.

Shanna brought one leg up and tucked it underneath her other leg. "If you could do anything, what would it be?" she asked. She was curious to hear his answer.

"Anything at all?" He scratched his neck.

"Yeah? Anything. Anywhere. No limits." She turned in her seat so she could watch him as he answered.

After a minute or so, he said, "I'd climb Mt. Everest."

"Seriously?" That wasn't what she expected.

"Yeah." He rested his right hand on his lap and drove with his left hand. "I'd love to scale that mountain and get to the top."

"Why don't you?" She could envision him hiking up the mountain.

"Too many responsibilities." He put his right hand back on the steering wheel.

She straightened in her seat. "You know, you've claimed I'm a workaholic and need to take time to enjoy things. Maybe you should take your own advice and do something you really want to do."

After a long silence, he said, "Maybe you're right. Maybe, someday,

I'll make it to Mt. Everest." He glanced at her. "What about you? What would you do?"

"Oh, that's easy," she said, "I'd sing in Carnegie Hall."

"Really?" He jerked his head back. "You sing?"

"Yeah. Not as well as I'd like, but if we're dreaming." She shrugged, then laughed. "I was in musicals in high school, and I wrote a few songs that I played on the piano. There's still a part of me that would love to perform somewhere like that."

"You should go for it." He smiled at her. "Really." His enthusiasm was more encouragement than Greg had ever given her.

"Well, now, I don't . . ." she stopped before she could finish. She didn't want to say she didn't have time to pursue anything but her career, even though that was the truth. She didn't think of herself as a workaholic. And yet she spent most of her time working and trying to secure a promotion. She was scheduled out every single day, even the weekends.

Her phone buzzed. She looked at the screen. It was her boss. "Hello?"

"Can you send me the final images for Waterbury Financial?" Renae sounded like she was on edge. But then she almost always sounded that way.

Shanna tensed as she said, "I, uh, can't right now." She didn't want to let her boss down or seem unprofessional.

"Why not?" Renae said it in such a way that Shanna felt like she was being accused of something.

She cleared her throat and said, "I'm currently on the road."

"I thought you were going to get there last night and would be available today. I need those final images."

"I know, but my car broke down and I stayed in a small town with limited internet." It was all true, but it sounded like she was making excuses for herself. And if there was something that Renae detested, it was that.

"Sounds like a lot of excuses, Shanna. You know how I feel about that."

"Yes, I do. I'll email you as soon as I get to Amarillo." Shanna hoped that would appease her.

"Send me the schedule for the media campaign for Waterbury as well."

"You'll have the images and the schedule," Shanna said, crossing her fingers.

"I'll see you on Monday," Renae said, ending the call.

Shanna laid her head back and took a few breaths to calm her nerves.

"Your boss again?" Cole said.

"Yep. I need to send her some stuff. And I need to be back in Denver on Monday morning." She massaged her temples.

"But your car won't be fixed until Monday afternoon." Cole glanced at her.

"Yeah. I'll have to figure something out." She wasn't sure what, but she'd have to be at work Monday or Renae might unconsider—if that was even a word—giving Shanna a promotion.

"What made you want to go into public relations?" Cole said, breaking into her thoughts.

"Oh, I helped my dad with some campaigns to build community awareness when I was a teenager and I enjoyed it. I went to Texas A&M. Majoring in Communications seemed to make sense, especially when my parents strongly encouraged it. At the time, I think my dad expected me to come work for him at the dealership when I graduated."

"Public Relations is what you've always wanted to do?" Cole said, his question piercing her. No one had ever asked her this before.

After a few moments of thought, she said, "I guess I wouldn't say that." Her career made sense and she was good at it. She was productive and delivered on time. She liked to influence and persuade others using her words and images in campaigns and wanted to help businesses improve their images, but if she were being completely honest, it wasn't her passion.

"What would you say?" Cole asked. "What career would you rather have?"

Talking to Cole made her dig deep and think about things she normally didn't. "I don't think I've ever voiced this before." She'd had thoughts ping pong around her mind, but she'd never given them much credence.

Cole didn't say anything.

After a few minutes of trying to put her thoughts into words, she said, "I'd thought here and there about becoming a high school choir teacher."

"Really?"

"I love singing. You know, my fantasy of performing at Carnegie Hall and all that." She laughed. "My choir teacher was amazing. She was so kind and inspirational. I felt like she truly cared about me and believed in me. I'd love to do that. I'd like to feel like I contribute something important to the universe."

"And you don't feel like you do that with public relations?"

"No. Not really. I mean, I help businesses, which is important, and I like what I do, but teaching kids to believe in themselves? Teaching them to express themselves through music? That impacts their lives. Teachers can have such a positive effect on kids."

"Sounds like you're passionate about this," he said.

"I guess I am." She hadn't thought seriously about pursuing teaching until this moment.

Cole shook his head.

"What?" She pulled her eyebrows together.

He shifted his weight in his seat. "You aren't what I expected."

"What does that mean?" she asked.

Cole cleared his throat. "When I picked you up yesterday, I pegged you for a busy, very determined but not-too-interested-in-anyone-else kind of a person."

"You mean self-centered?" she said, feeling offended, but also realizing he was right. She didn't think too much of other people. She was focused on herself and her career and that was basically it.

"Uh . . . no . . . I . . . I guess that came out wrong," he said stumbling all over his words.

Shanna gazed out the window. "I am determined and intense at times. I tend to get laser-focused on my projects and my career."

"That's not a bad thing," he said. "I'm sorry, I didn't mean to—"

"No apology necessary." She said with a wave of her hand. "You're right. It isn't a bad thing, but it does make it hard to connect with other people." Other than her assistant, Kaylie, Shanna didn't really have many friends, because she spent most of her time working. She had to admit it, she was a workaholic.

Cole gave her a sideways glance. "We seem to be connecting. Don't you think?"

A smile crept across her mouth. "Yeah. You're very easy to talk to," Shanna said.

"Back at ya," he said.

After a few moments, she asked, "Did you always want to study law?" She was curious about this man who'd drawn so much out of her on this drive.

"No. I planned to run the ranch." He adjusted his hat.

"What made you want to be an attorney?" She assumed it wasn't because he wanted to make a lot of money—that didn't seem to be his style.

"My senior year of high school, my grandpa was driving home after a Farm Bureau meeting in Denver when he was hit by a drunk driver."

"Oh, no." She covered her mouth, sadness washing over her. "Your mom's dad?"

Nodding, Cole went on, "It was a terrible accident, and he didn't survive. But the other driver did."

"I'm so sorry. That's awful." Shanna's throat felt thick.

"And the guy had a great lawyer who got him off with a couple of years and community service since it was his first offense." Cole clenched his jaw.

"That doesn't seem right." How unfair that his grandpa died, and the drunk driver survived.

"That's what I thought. So, after some deliberation, I decided to study law and make sure justice was served." He gave a firm nod.

"Has it been?"

"I think so. At least in my small corner of the world," he said.

They drove for several minutes in silence while Shanna contemplated their conversation. In another time and place, she'd want to spend more time with Cole. She enjoyed talking to him and there was a definite connection between them. She had to be realistic. Suddenly, an idea popped into her head.

"I appreciate you driving me," she said.

"You've mentioned that." He gave her a quick look and smiled, which made her stomach quiver.

Drawing in a breath, she said, "Do you need to get right back tonight?"

"What are you suggesting?" he said in a playful tone.

"I was thinking maybe you'd stay for the dinner and dance." It sounded a little crazy considering they'd only met yesterday, but she wasn't ready to say goodbye yet.

"Hmm." He said it as if he was pondering the idea.

"My parents have a couple of spare bedrooms. You could get an early start in the morning. Just an idea." She didn't want him to think it was a big deal. Because it wasn't a big deal if he wanted to turn right around and go back home, but she hoped he'd agree to stay.

"I wouldn't want to impose on your parents' celebration."

"After you driving me all the way to Amarillo? My parents will have nothing but gratitude for you, believe me." She knew her parents would both be so happy he brought her in time for the celebration.

"Sounds like an offer I can't refuse," he said.

"Great." Shanna leaned her head back against the seat, trying to contain the smile exploding across her face.

CHAPTER 9

Shanna jerked awake. "Oh, no. I didn't mean to fall asleep."

"No problem," Cole said. He was happy she'd gotten a little rest. She seemed stressed about her job.

"How long was I asleep?" She gazed out the window. "Because we're close."

"According to my GPS, we're about a mile or so from your house." He was glad she'd given him her address, so he didn't have to disturb her while she was sleeping.

Shanna smoothed her hair and wiped at her face.

"Beautiful neighborhood." This area was drastically different from where he'd grown up.

Shanna nodded.

"Do you miss Amarillo?" he said as he turned left.

"Sometimes. It'll always be my hometown. Lots of memories here, but my home is in Denver now."

Cole made another turn.

"The Morrisons finally painted their house. It used to be this ugly green color," she said as they drove past houses. "Turn right at this corner," she said, pointing ahead.

They drove down a tree-lined street with large, two-story homes.

When he came to a circular driveway in front of a white, colonial style home with pillars in front, she said, "This is it."

He nodded as he gazed at the large house with trees on either side and a gazebo peeking out from behind the fence. Owning a car dealership must have its perks.

"You can pull in right by the front door."

Cole parked the truck and they exited. Shanna pulled a key from her purse and opened the front door. "Hello? Is anyone home?"

No one answered.

"I'm not sure where they are. They had a brunch earlier, but I thought they'd be home by now," Shanna said.

Cole stood in front of the circular staircase. He gazed at the exquisite cut glass chandelier that hung above them and then down at the marble tiles in the entryway. Not much like the farmhouse he'd called home.

"I'll text my mom and see where they are," Shanna said, stepping out of her shoes. "I didn't want to tell her we were getting close until we actually got here."

"I'm happy to take you wherever they are." He admired a painting that hung on the wall of a log home surrounded by a forest.

After a few minutes, Shanna said, "They're at the zoo with my brother's family."

"I'll take you." Cole didn't want her to miss out on any of the activities.

"That's so nice of you. By the time we got there, though, they'd be done and on their way to a couple's massage." Shanna set her phone down on the entry table and stretched. "Let's freshen up here." She gazed at him with her mesmerizing blue eyes. "You'll come to the dinner and dance?"

Cole patted his jeans. "I'm not really dressed for an event like that." He'd planned to drive her to Amarillo, then turn around and go back to Juniper Springs, so he didn't have a change of clothes.

"That's not an issue," Shanna said with a smile that tugged at his heart.

"I can't go dressed in my jeans and t-shirt." He may have been from the country, but he knew he needed much nicer attire for the kind of dinner and dance they'd be attending.

"We can go shopping." She stepped closer to him.

"Shopping?" He'd rather chew on cactus than have to go to a store and shop.

"Sure. I'll buy you a suit." She said it so jovially, he almost thought it could be fun. But then he remembered that shopping was even less fun than chasing a loose bull looking for love.

"Uh, no," he said as nicely as possible.

"You don't like suits?"

"I don't like shopping."

She shook her head. "Such a man thing to say. Come on. It'll be fun."

He raised a finger in the air. "One. Shopping and fun don't belong in the same sentence." He added another finger. "And, two, I'm not going to have you buy me a suit."

Shanna started walking toward a hallway. Over her shoulder, she said, "It's the least I can do. It's my way of saying thank you for driving me here. Then you'll be ready for the dinner and dance."

He followed her down the hall. "I can buy my own suit."

She turned and walked backward as she said, "Come on. Let me do this for you. I know the perfect place."

They entered the massive kitchen with marble counters and sleek white cabinets. The appliances were all stainless steel. Shanna opened a cabinet and pulled out two glasses.

"But—"

Before he could say anything else, Shanna said, "You've never been shopping with me." She set the glasses down.

"That's true."

She opened the oversized refrigerator and pulled out a glass pitcher of orange juice. "Fresh squeezed. Want some?"

"Sure." He could never say no to orange juice.

She poured the juice into the glasses, then set the pitcher on the counter. "I need a new dress."

"You didn't bring one?" How could she have come for a fancy celebration and not brought a dress?

"I did, but I don't really like it." She took a sip of orange juice.

"You brought a dress you don't like?" That didn't make any sense to him.

"Well, I was too busy to get one."

He nodded. That made more sense. "I believe that." He sipped his juice.

"Do you want to go to the bedroom?" Shanna asked.

He sputtered and coughed. "Huh?"

Shanna made a cringey face. "That came out *so* wrong." She shook her head. "I meant, do you want me to take you to the guest room?"

"I don't really have any stuff. Remember?"

"Oh, yeah." She slapped herself on the forehead. "Are you hungry?"

"I could eat something." His stomach grumbled whenever anyone mentioned food.

Shanna walked back to the fridge. "There's usually plenty to snack on in here. There are some grapes. Cheese. I could make you a charcuterie board."

"A char-whatery board?" He'd never heard of that word.

She waved her hand. "What about a sandwich?"

"Thanks. A sandwich sounds great." He could eat a sandwich any time of day.

Shanna pulled out some meat, cheese, and gourmet mustard. "After you eat this, we'll go shop for a suit for you and a dress for me," she said brightly.

Cole wasn't sure what he'd gotten himself into. Shopping was like slow torture but spending more time with Shanna was too appealing to say no. He knew it was probably better for him to hop back in his truck and drive home—that was what he should do, but it wasn't what he wanted to do. Against his better judgment, he decided to stay.

"Oh, look at this charcoal suit," Shanna said, pulling it from the display rack. Imagining Cole wearing it sent a tingle down her back.

"Nice." He touched the sleeve.

"It'd look good on you." Of course, anything would look amazing on him. She reminded herself that this was a gift for driving her to Amarillo and nothing else. The *nothing else* part was getting harder and harder for her to remember. "Try on the jacket."

Cole tried it on, and it was a perfect fit. Shanna tamped down the desire to hold him in her arms. *Stop. Now. Get a hold of yourself.*

"It fits. But I can't let you buy me a suit."

"Yes, you can. You spent your time driving me almost four hours and I want to say thank you. You don't have a problem with someone saying thank you, do you?" There. She had him. He'd have to accept the suit.

"Well, no, but—"

"No buts. This suit will look great. We need a shirt and tie."

Cole held his hand up as if to protest, but Shanna ignored him.

"You can't very well come to my parents' party dressed in a suit with no shirt or tie." She refused to let any thoughts of Cole being shirtless enter her head.

"Yes, but—"

"Oh, this silver tie will look amazing." Shanna handed him the silk tie. She walked over to a rack of dress shirts and picked out a blue one. "And this one. I think this is your size."

"You know, I have suits and shirts and ties back home," he said.

"You can add this to your wardrobe. Maybe you'll remember me when you're arguing a case and wearing this suit." She smiled, hoping he wouldn't forget her because she knew she wasn't ever going to forget him.

"I'm pretty sure I'll remember you," he said with a sparkle in his magnetic eyes.

They went over to the desk and Shanna paid for the items. Cole tried to resist, but she reminded him this was her way of saying thank you.

"What about a dress for you?" he said.

"Over here," she said, pointing to another area of the large department store.

They walked over to a display of some formal dresses. Shanna rummaged through them. She picked out a blue beaded gown. "I'll try this one on."

She went into the dressing room and tried on the dress. It hugged her curves in all the right places and made her feel like she was royalty. She spun around in front of the mirror. This was exactly the kind of dress she'd hoped to find for tonight. After a few moments of evaluating herself, she went out to show Cole.

As she walked out, she noticed his eyes widen and she smiled to herself. "Oh, uh . . . that dress . . . looks . . . good . . . very nice . . . on you," he said, tripping over his words.

"Does it?" she said, fishing for more compliments.

"Yeah. Looks like it was made special for you," he said, smiling in a way that let her know he found her attractive.

She was in dangerous territory, but she hadn't felt like this in a long time, and she decided it was okay to enjoy it. She was seizing the moment and it felt good. Being with Cole felt good.

Shanna's phone rang. She rushed back to her dressing room to grab it. "Hi, Mom," she said, trying to hide her giddiness.

"Where are you?" her mom asked.

"We're at Dillard's." She twirled around and gazed at herself in the three-way mirror right outside the dressing room.

"Why?"

"Why what?" She'd forgotten what her mom asked.

"Shanna?"

"Yes?"

"What's going on?" her mom said suspiciously.

Focusing back on the phone call, Shanna said, "Oh, uh, nothing. I didn't have a chance to get a new dress before I came, so Cole and I have been shopping. He needed a suit for tonight."

"Tonight?"

"Yes, I invited him to the party."

"You did?" Her mom sounded *something*, but she couldn't put her finger on it.

"Is that a problem?" Shanna said quietly. She couldn't imagine why it would be a problem to invite him after he drove her all the way home.

"No, no. It's fine. No worries at all. It'll be fine." Her mom seemed to be overly gracious. "Are you headed back to the house now?"

"As soon as I buy this dress," Shanna said. "Will you be there?"

"We're on our way home now," her mom said.

"We'll see you soon," Shanna said, then ended the call and walked back out to where Cole was standing.

"Your mom?" he asked.

"Yes. They're on their way back." Shanna admired her dress in the mirror again.

"I really don't want to impose on your party," he said.

"You aren't." She turned and looked directly at him. "Your mom made me feel so comfortable while I was in Juniper Springs. It's my turn to make you feel comfortable here." She wanted to reassure him.

He plunged his hands into his pockets. "I appreciate that, but this is still your family party."

Shanna laughed. "Half of Amarillo will be there. Believe me, this is a big party. I think my dad might be telling people that he's thinking about running for an office in state government."

"He must have liked being the mayor," Cole said.

"Oh, he did. I think this party is serving a few purposes." She twirled around in the dress again. "Yes, on this dress?"

Cole nodded. "Definitely."

CHAPTER 10

*O*n the way back over to the house, Shanna and Cole chatted. The conversation was so easy with him. There weren't any awkward lulls or weird vibes. It was like they'd known each other for years.

"You can park in the same place as before," Shanna directed Cole.

"It won't be blocking anyone?" he asked. Shanna appreciated that he was so considerate.

"No." Shanna knew her parents parked their cars in the garage. No one ever parked in the driveway unless there were visitors.

They got out of the truck and walked into the house carrying their packages. This time there were voices and movement inside the house.

"Shanna? Is that you?" said her mom, who was wearing a wide smile. She rushed over to Shanna and enveloped her into a big hug. "I'm so glad you made it."

"Of course." Shanna wanted to be here to celebrate their thirty years together.

"I was so worried when you said your car broke down," her mom said still holding her tight.

Shanna pulled away. "Thankfully, Cole here came to the rescue."
She gestured to him.

"You're the tow truck driver?" her mom said as she eyed Cole.

He dipped his head and smiled. "Uh, yes."

"Thank you so much." She extended her hand and shook Cole's.
"Thank you for towing her car and then going above and beyond and
driving her all the way here. Quite magnanimous of you."

"I'm glad I could assist," Cole said. Shanna couldn't help but admire
how genuine he was. There was no pretense about him at all.

"I'll take him up to the guest bedroom so he can change for the
party," Shanna said.

A strange expression crossed her mom's face. Shanna studied her
mom, then said, "What?"

"Oh, nothing. That's a good idea." Her mom brushed it off, but
Shanna suspected something was going on.

Shanna motioned for Cole to follow her up the stairs. They
entered the guest room. "You can use this room. The bathroom is over
there."

"Thanks." He set his garment bag with the suit inside on the bed.

"We have a little while before we need to leave for the party. You
can hang out up here or come back downstairs." Shanna hoped he'd
choose the latter.

She left Cole in the room. As she walked down the hall, she let
some thoughts circle around her mind. Thoughts that centered on her
and Cole getting to know each other and exploring a relationship. She
shook her head and laughed to herself. She'd only met the man
yesterday when he towed her car. *Yesterday.* How could she possibly
entertain any thoughts like these? It was silly.

CHAPTER 11

ole sat on the four-poster bed with the white lace bedspread. The room was pink and had a crystal chandelier hanging from the center. A gold-leaf mirror hung on the wall and lace curtains adorned the windows. It was definitely a frilly room. He went into the bathroom with its marble counter and tile floor. He leaned onto his hands on the counter and gazed at himself in the large mirror. What was he doing?

He'd volunteered to drive a woman he hardly knew four hours to a city he'd never been to. He agreed to stay for a lavish party. And then he'd allowed her to buy him a suit. He'd never done anything like this before.

From the second he'd met her Friday evening, he'd felt a little off kilter. He'd met women before, but this woman was different. Shanna made him feel things he hadn't felt in a long time. He couldn't explain it, except that she made him feel alive. Excited. Enthusiastic. For a moment, he let himself consider what his life might be like with Shanna in it.

He walked back into the bedroom and sat on the bed. Maybe in a different time or a different place, he and Shanna would have had a chance, but as it was, this would all end as fast as it began.

For the moment, though, he was here. He had a new suit. And he was going to be spending the evening with her. If that's all it would ever be, he'd take it.

~

"Isn't it strange for a man you don't even know to attend the party?" her mom asked as they stood in the kitchen.

Shanna countered, "Do you know everyone who's going to attend tonight?"

"Of course," her mom said. She started rearranging flowers in a vase that stood atop the marble island.

Shanna gave her mom a skeptical look.

With a white carnation in her hand, her mom said, "All right, so your father might have invited some people I don't know very well. But that's different." She pushed the carnation into the arrangement.

"Why?" Shanna wanted her mom to explain herself because she was acting so odd.

"Shanna, I want you to enjoy the party. That's all." She gave Shanna a quick smile.

Walking around the island and sitting on the barstool, Shanna said, "I will. Cole is a great guy."

"But there's no future with him." She peered at Shanna.

Future? She'd barely met the man. She didn't think there was a future either, but not for the same reasons. "Why? Because he's a tow truck driver?"

"No. I wasn't thinking that," her mom said.

"Mom, you are so transparent." Shanna shook her head.

"You're both very different. You are—"

Shanna held up her hand. "You can save your worries, Mom. There is nothing between us. He's a nice guy who offered to bring me here. The least I could do is invite him for dinner. There's nothing more to it than that." She wasn't sure if she was trying to convince her mom or herself.

With an arched eyebrow, her mom said, "I don't know about that."

"Huh?" What did her mom mean?

She took some greenery and placed it in the vase. "That there's nothing between you. It seems like there's something."

"I promise, there isn't." Even as the words came out of her mouth, she struggled to believe them.

"I'm grateful he brought you. It's kind of you to think of him and invite him to the party." Her mom finished arranging the flowers. She collected some cut stems and placed them in the garbage.

"That's all it is." She wasn't sure why her mom was so concerned about it.

"Shanna," her dad said as he walked into the kitchen looking handsome in his gray dress shirt.

"Hi, Daddy." She gave him a hug.

"What's happening with your car?"

"It needs a water pump." She nodded. "Hopefully, it will be fixed Monday."

He slung his arm around her shoulders. "You know, if you'd take one of the cars from the lot you wouldn't have these problems."

"I know. I appreciate it, Dad. But I love my car," she said, holding her ground. She needed to prove she could stand on her own two feet.

He stepped back. "You're so independent."

Not wanting to discuss her independence, including moving to Denver, yet again, she said, "How about this awesome party? I can't wait to see the two of you all dressed up and enjoying your celebration."

"We're excited for it," her mom said.

"Where is Patrick?" Her dad gazed around the kitchen.

"He and Lacey took the boys home to get ready for the celebration," her mom said.

"I can't wait to see my nephews. I bet they've both grown so much." Every time Shanna came to visit, she marveled at how much taller the boys were.

"I wish you'd get a job closer to home. I don't know what you see in Denver," her mom said with a sad expression.

Shanna wanted to defend her choice to move to Colorado, but she didn't want to make her mom feel bad. "I love living there. But I do miss you and Dad and I'm going to try to come home more often." She hoped that would appease her mom.

Enveloping her in a hug, her mom said, "I'm selfish and want to see my daughter more. We missed you at the brunch and the zoo." Her mom stepped back.

"The boys loved the snakes." She shuddered.

Shanna laughed thinking of her mom's dislike for all reptiles in general. "We really tried to get here sooner. I'm sorry we missed it."

"I'm glad you're here now," her mom said, then glanced up at the clock on the wall. "Oh, I need to go make myself presentable. I'm wearing a new silver dress." She smiled.

"This will be a great party," Shanna said.

CHAPTER 12

*S*hanna finished the last touches of her makeup, then smoothed her hair. She wanted to feel beautiful tonight. Not for anyone in particular, of course. She was excited to see Patrick. It had been almost a year since she'd been home and seen him. Time seemed to fly by too fast.

She left her bedroom and walked along the hallway. At the bottom of the stairs, she could see Cole. As she descended the stairs, he turned, and her breath caught. He looked incredible in his new suit, shirt, and tie. Her heart skittered with each step she took.

"Hi," she said when she got to the bottom. "You clean up well." That was the understatement of the year.

"Thank you." He gave her a half-smile as he dipped his head, then said, "You look even more beautiful now than when you tried this dress on."

Her cheeks warmed. "Thank you."

"Are you ready?" he said.

"Yes." She gazed around. "Where are my parents?"

"They left a little while ago."

"I'm not surprised. Punctuality is important to my dad. He thinks if you're less than twenty minutes early, then you're late." She nodded. "It was a big source of contention growing up."

"Oh yeah?"

"My teenage self needed lots of time to get ready for school and church and other events, which drove my dad crazy." She could almost hear her dad's familiar whistle that meant it was time to get in the car.

"I never had a sister, so I guess I missed out on that." He chuckled.

Cole extended his arm. "May I escort you to the truck?" He cleared his throat. "Or maybe it'd be better to say that your carriage awaits," he said, his eyes twinkling.

"As long as you don't call me ma'am."

He held up his hand. "I wasn't going to."

"You weren't?" She eyed him.

With a small shrug, he said, "At least I caught myself *before* I said it."

"You get points for that." She patted him on the arm.

"And if I get a lot of points, then what?" He gazed at her, and it made the tips of her ears warm.

Twirling a piece of her hair, she said, "I guess we'll see."

They walked out to the truck, and he helped her in. She didn't need help, but she didn't mind his hand on the small of her back as she got into the cab.

They began driving to the event.

"I'll be at a big disadvantage tonight because I won't know anyone," Cole said.

"How about I introduce you to the people I know? I'm pretty sure there will be a lot of people I don't know." She could only imagine how many people her parents had invited to this gala.

"It's really sweet you came all this way to support your parents," he said.

"I couldn't have done it without you." If anyone had gone above and beyond, it was Cole. He'd made a huge effort to help someone he didn't even know. "Thank you."

"You're most welcome."

～

THEY ARRIVED at the Bluebonnet Hotel and Convention Center and parked the truck.

"This is a nice place," Cole said, gazing at the large glass building with trees surrounding it.

"My dad loves this hotel," she said, recalling events she'd attended here.

They walked into the lobby, which was decorated in gray colors with framed photos of bluebonnet flowers, the Texas flag, and Amarillo sunsets. A large sign with Lyndley Anniversary Party stood on an easel.

"May I help you?" asked a young woman with black hair wrapped tightly into a bun.

"We're here for the anniversary party," Shanna said, pointing at the sign.

"It's down that hall in the Primrose Room." She gestured to a hallway to their right.

"Thank you," Shanna said. They walked into the Primrose Room and Shanna gasped. It had been transformed into a magical space with strings and strings of mini lights. Flower arrangements were scattered throughout the room. A live band was at the other end and there was a table with hors d'oeuvres.

"There's my brother," Shanna said. Excitement welled up as she made her way over to him.

She threw her arms around Patrick's neck. "So good to see you," she said.

"It's been a while," he said as he pulled away. "I'm glad you made it. Mom was pretty stressed."

"I know," Shanna said. "Oh, Patrick, this is Cole."

Patrick put his hand out and Cole shook it. "Nice to meet you," her brother said.

"You, too."

"Thanks for bringing Shanna here safe and sound. It means a lot," he said with a nod.

Cole smiled.

"Do you need help with anything?" Shanna asked.

"I don't think so." Patrick shrugged.

"I'm so sorry I wasn't here to help," Shanna said. The truth was, she was too busy to help with her parents' anniversary party. She was too busy for anything but work. That was her life. And she liked it that way. Didn't she?

"Don't worry about it. Lacey and I got it." Patrick said the words, but Shanna could tell there was some resentment.

"How's working at the dealership?" she asked.

"It's going well."

Lacey approached them, her long black hair cascading down her back. "Hi, Shanna."

"Hi, Lacey."

They embraced. Shanna loved her sister-in-law, even if they didn't spend much time together.

"So glad you made it." Lacey turned to Cole. "And you must be the knight in shining armor." She laughed.

Cole shook his head. "I did what needed to be done." Shanna might have just met Cole, but she knew he wasn't one for accolades.

"You're too humble. You totally saved the day bringing her here." Lacey looked at Shanna and shielded her mouth as she said, "And he's so handsome."

Ignoring the warmth that crept up her neck, she said, "Good to see you. This all looks amazing. I was asking Patrick if you needed any help."

"I think it's all ready. I love parties so much," Lacey said with a wide grin.

"That's why you're such a great event planner," Shanna said.

Lacey clasped her hands together. "Thanks. It's so fun."

"You did a wonderful job here." Shanna gazed around the elegantly decorated room.

"I'm going to check on some things in the kitchen," Lacey said. "Patrick, can you help me?"

Shanna's brother shrugged and followed his wife. "Your brother and his wife are awesome," Cole said.

"Yeah. I was so happy when they got married. Lacey is super fun. And I have the cutest nephews in the world." She couldn't wait to see the boys.

"Hello, Shanna. Good to see you," Irene Whitley, a long-time employee at the Ford dealership, said.

"Hi, Irene. Good to see you." Shanna nodded. Irene still had the flaming red hair she remembered, plus a few extra wrinkles. "This is Cole."

He said, "Good to meet you, Irene."

"Nice to meet you. I've known Shanna since she was a little girl," she said. "You make a lovely couple. How long have you been dating?" She touched Shanna on the arm. "Or are you engaged already? Things happen so fast these days."

"Oh," Shanna said, jerking her head back. "We aren't engaged." A nervous laugh fell out of her mouth. "We... aren't ... even a couple."

"You aren't?" Irene blinked, then scrunched her eyebrows together. "So sorry. My mistake. I thought, I mean, looking at the two of you together. I assumed. I'm sorry," Irene said, her cheeks blushing.

"No problem at all," Cole said in a sincere tone.

Irene gave a quick wave, then scooted away.

"I'm so sorry. Irene has worked at the dealership for a million years," Shanna said, feeling flushed herself. Why had Irene assumed they were a couple?

"No need to apologize," he said. "I don't mind."

"You don't mind if people think we're a couple?" Was he okay with the idea? If he was okay with it, was she?

He simply smiled in that Cole kind of way that made Shanna's heart flutter.

"We should find a seat," Shanna said, trying to stay focused on the event and not on Cole or the way he made her feel all light and floaty.

"I'm right behind you," he said.

They walked toward a table.

"Shanna." It was her mom's voice.

"Hi, Mom," she said as she turned around.

Her mom eyed Cole. For some reason, it seemed like she didn't want Cole to come. Was it because he was basically a stranger? Did her mom get a weird vibe from him? "We have seats over here," she said, pointing to a table at the front of the room. She gazed around the room.

Shanna studied her mom, who seemed to be looking for someone.

"Are you looking for Dad?"

"Oh, uh . . . yes. For your dad. Have you seen him?"

"Mom? You're acting a little weird. Are you okay?" Shanna said.

"Of course. I'm fine. Better than fine." She smiled, then walked away.

Shanna leaned in and said, "My mom usually isn't so . . . strange. I'm sure it's because she's nervous. That's it. She's acting nervous, don't you think?" It was the only explanation.

"That's possible," Cole said. "This is a big event."

"I wonder if my dad is going to announce his candidacy or something. Maybe she's looking for reporters." It was all beginning to make sense now.

"What office is he going to run for?" Cole said, keeping his gaze on Shanna.

"State something. . . I can't remember." Shanna didn't keep track of everything going on with her family since she was so immersed in her own life, which only meant she was consumed with her job.

"Maybe we should find a seat," Cole said.

"That's a good idea." Shanna turned. "Oh, no." Long-buried feelings bubbled to the surface.

Pulling his eyebrows together, he asked, "What is it?"

"Over there." She inclined her head to her left while memories rushed in.

"What am I looking at?" Cole seemed to be quite confused.

As discreetly as possible, Shanna pointed to her old nemesis, Amelia Cook.

"The woman in the red dress?"

"Yes. But don't stare at her." Shanna turned her back toward Amelia. "I knew her in high school. She tried to steal my boyfriend. I can't believe she's here." Amelia was the very last person she wanted to see.

"Tell me when she's gone." Shanna planned to avoid her at all costs. She shaded her face with her hand and said, "But don't look at her."

"How will I be able to tell you she's gone if I don't look?" Cole said.

"Okay. But don't be obvious." Shanna sounded like a crazy person, which wasn't surprising. Amelia made her straight-up nuts. "Is she gone?"

"I haven't looked yet."

"Now?"

Cole gazed nonchalantly in that direction. "Uh, oh."

"What do you mean, 'uh, oh.' Why did you say that?" Shanna was losing it. She was acting like she was back in high school instead of a grown, independent, career woman.

"I—"

"Oh, Shanna, there you are. Your dad said you were coming," came the familiar nails-on-chalkboard voice. One that Shanna never wanted to hear again. But there she was, and Shanna had to respond in the most mature way she could.

Reluctantly, Shanna turned and with a pasted-on smile said, "My dad?" When did Amelia see her dad?

"Yeah. I've been working at the dealership for the last year," she said in her Amelia way.

"You have?" Her dad had hired Amelia Cook, of all people. Was there some kind of employee shortage in Amarillo and her dad was so desperate he'd hired Amelia?

Amelia fluffed her straightened brown hair. "I'm in the sales department. I'm surprised your parents didn't tell you. They're the best ever." She chortled.

"Never came up, I guess." Shanna let out a long breath. This night was not turning out the way she'd hoped.

"Well, how have you been?" Amelia said.

"Good, good. You?" Shanna didn't want to have a conversation with Amelia, but she couldn't be rude.

"Very well." She turned to Cole and touched him on the shoulder, which brought back an avalanche of memories, all of them bad. "And who might you be?"

"This is Cole," Shanna said, trying to remember they weren't in high school anymore.

Amelia eyed him up and down and it made Shanna want to scream. "Hello." Amelia gave him a smirk that Shanna was sure Amelia thought was sexy, but it was simply comical instead. Watching the whole thing made Shanna feel like she was in a time warp.

"Hi." Cole gave her a sincere smile because Cole was a good guy through and through. Did he even know how to be insincere?

"How did you two meet?" Amelia took a stance that seemed more like a pose.

"Oh, it's a long story. I'm sure you don't want to listen to all of it," Shanna said.

Amelia arched an eyebrow. "If you say so. Nice to meet you, Cole." The way she said it made Shanna's nerves explode. How dare she try to slither up to Cole.

"Likewise," he said.

After Amelia walked away, Cole said, "Feels like we're in the North Pole."

"She makes me so mad." Shanna rolled her eyes. "How could my father have hired her?"

Cole watched her.

"I'm sorry. You don't need to get sucked into high school drama from years ago." Shanna wanted to slap herself for letting Amelia get under her skin.

Whispering behind the back of his hand, he said, "I think we all have Amelias."

Add *empathetic* to the long list of Cole's attributes. Whoever ended up with him would be a lucky woman indeed.

Patrick held a microphone and began speaking. "Welcome everyone. We're honored that you've come to celebrate my parents' anniversary tonight. We have some great food coming and then we'll get to dance to the music of The Armadillos. Please find a seat so we can begin with dinner."

Cole and Shanna took their seats at her parents' table.

A woman dressed in a white shirt and black pants approached the table with a tray of plates. As she neared the table, she started to lose her grip on the tray. In a flash, Cole was up and securing the tray for her.

"Oh my gosh. I'm so sorry," she said. "Thank you!"

"Glad I could help."

"My boss would yell at me for sure if I'd dropped these plates on y'all."

"No harm, no foul," Cole said.

She set the tray down, then grabbed the plates and placed them in front of Cole and Shanna.

"Thank you," Shanna said to the server. She glanced across the table at her mom who wore a disapproving expression. "Things like this happen to all of us. Don't worry about it." She didn't want her to feel bad for a simple, almost very messy, mistake.

The server set plates in front of Shanna's parents and her brother and his wife.

"This looks delicious," Cole said.

"You like salad?" Shanna asked.

"It's not my favorite, but this one looks good."

Shanna admired his diplomacy.

They finished the salads in time for the server to bring chicken cordon bleu.

As they began eating, Shanna said, "That was a nice thing you did for the server."

He sat back. "It was selfish, actually."

"Because you didn't want to wear the first course?" she said.

"Exactly. I don't look very good in a salad shirt."

Shanna laughed.

"Cole," her dad said from across the table. "What is it that you do?"

"Yes, sir. I am an attorney, but currently I'm helping my mother run our inn, the ranch, and our garage."

"You aren't a tow truck driver?" her mom asked, kitting her brows together.

"Occasionally. We have a driver, but he was out for the night. I took over to help out and that's when Shanna's call came in." He took a bite of his chicken.

"You're an attorney?" she said.

Cole nodded.

Shanna gave her mom a you-shouldn't-have-made-a-rash-judgment smile.

"You grew up in . . ." her dad said, circling his fork in the air.

"Juniper Springs, Colorado," Cole said.

"Colorado is a beautiful state," her mom said. "We've been skiing up in Breckenridge. That's when Shanna fell in love with Colorado. I didn't think she'd move there, though."

Shanna bit back what she wanted to say because this was a conversation they'd had too many times.

"Where is Juniper Springs?" Patrick asked.

"It's on I-25 south of Denver a few hours. It's a small town," Cole said.

"I've probably passed it when I've driven up to Denver." Patrick took a bite of his mashed potatoes.

"If you blink, you'll miss it." Cole laughed.

"But it's a great town," Shanna said. "Their inn is right on the river and the rooms are all so charming. And there's a super adorable downtown area. We went dancing," Shanna said.

"Sounds like you enjoyed it," her dad said.

"I guess if your car is going to break down, Juniper Springs is the best place to do it." Shanna laughed.

Her mom's attention was on the other side of the room.

"Mom?" Shanna said.

"Yes?"

"Who are you looking for now?" Shanna asked pointedly.

Her mom blinked. "No one . . . Not anyone. I was . . . wondering who's here."

"There are a lot of people who showed up," her dad said.

"See, I told you. You have a lot of support. You should make a run for the senate." Her mom elbowed him.

Her dad nodded, then sipped his drink.

"This chicken is so good," Cole said.

"As good as Ada's?" Shanna said.

"Who is Ada?" Her mom asked.

"This very sweet woman who makes the most delicious food. She has this diner that is amazing." Shanna emphasized her words with her hands.

With raised eyebrows, her mom said. "Sounds like you're quite enamored of this little town."

"Like I said, it was a great place to break down." Shanna had planned to drive directly to Amarillo, but her car had other plans. She had to admit, she was happy it had worked out the way it did.

Lacey's phone rang. "It's the sitter. I hope the boys are okay." She answered the phone, then got up and walked away from the table.

"The boys are always getting into trouble. Last week, they both got into the flour because they wanted to make it *snow* in the living room and then they hid to see their mom's reaction. She wasn't pleased," Patrick said with wide eyes.

"What a mess," Shanna said.

Lacey returned to the table.

"Is everything all right?" Patrick asked.

"Yeah, they were trying to talk her into ordering pizza and watching that movie I've said they couldn't watch at least a hundred times."

He shook his head.

"Those boys are going to be the death of me." Lacey rubbed her temples.

"Remember, tonight we aren't worrying about the boys. We're enjoying dinner and dancing." Patrick caressed her arm.

"Easier said than done." She blew out a breath.

The server returned with dessert, which was cheesecake with strawberries on top.

"I love cheesecake," Cole said. He sank his fork into his piece.

Shanna watched as he ate the bite, savoring every moment of it. Cole seemed to enjoy the little things in life, something Shanna realized she needed to do more often.

"These strawberries are so sweet," Cole said.

Shanna smiled at him, then took a bite.

After they finished dessert, Shanna excused herself to go to the bathroom. Lacey followed her.

Inside the door, Lacey said with keen interest, "Tell me about this Cole guy."

Shanna smoothed her hair as she gazed at herself in the mirror. She checked to make sure she didn't have any food particles hiding between her teeth. "What do you want to know?"

"He seems like a fantastic guy." Lacey leaned against the counter.

"He is," Shanna said. Cole was the whole package—handsome, kind, thoughtful, considerate, excellent conversationalist, and fun.

"And?" Lacey said expectantly.

"Yes, he's a great guy. Yes, I enjoy being around him. Yes, he's easy to talk to. I feel like I know him better than people I've known a lot longer." What else could she say?

"You're falling for him," Lacey said, her eyes bright with enthusiasm.

Shanna straightened. "I barely met him."

Lacey fluttered her fingers. "Love at first sight. So romantic."

Laughing, Shanna said, "You should stop watching all those Hallmark movies."

"That isn't a denial," Lacey said.

Shanna turned and leaned against the counter next to Lacey. "Even if, say, I'd be interested in spending more time with him, it doesn't matter."

Lacey held her hands out in front of her. "Why not?"

"Because," she said, shrugging a shoulder. "We live in different places."

"Good thing there aren't phones that do like video calls. Oh, wait. There are." Lacey tapped her forehead.

Shaking her head, Shanna said, "I've already done the long-distance thing. It was an epic disaster, and I don't want to do it again."

"Maybe it wasn't the distance, but the guy."

"Maybe," Shanna said. Lacey had a point, but it still didn't matter. "We're also very different."

"Ooo. Love at first sight *and* opposites attract." Lacey clapped her hands together. "This is awesome."

Shanna stood and took a few steps away from the counter. "You don't get it. I'm a city girl and he's a country boy."

"That excuse is so cliché." Lacey waved her hands.

"It's cliché for a reason. Because it doesn't work." She was right. If the deck was stacked against them, what was the point?

Shanna walked out of the bathroom area and Lacey followed her.

"You like the city, and he likes the country. Okay. From where I was sitting, it sounds like you think where he lives is pretty amazing," Lacey said.

Shanna turned and faced her. "Maybe, but I would never live there." She couldn't see herself living in such a small town even if it was quaint. And sweet. And filled with kind people.

"Why not?" Lacey peered at her.

"Because. Because I love my job. I love my apartment." It was true. She was happy where she worked and lived.

Lacey placed her hands on Shanna's shoulders. "You love your single life?"

"Yes, actually. I do." She tried to punctuate that as much as possible so she could convince her sister-in-law that it was true. She did like being single. She did.

"Uh, huh." Lacey dropped her hands.

"Tomorrow he'll leave and that will be the end of it." Even as she said it, sadness shot through her. Was she ready to tell him goodbye?

Lacey crossed her arms in front of her chest. "Hmmm."

"What does that mean?"

"It means that there's obviously something between you." Lacey pointed at her.

"He's a good guy and that's the end of it," Shanna said as convincingly as possible.

"All right. If you say so," Lacey said.

Shanna gave her a nod. "I do."

CHAPTER 13

*S*hanna returned to the table. It had been cleared off and the lighting dimmed. At the front of the room, her brother stepped over to a microphone. "Thank you, everyone, for coming tonight. It means a lot to my parents. Please, make sure you sign the guest book. They want to keep track of their friends and family who shared this evening with them."

"They met back in college at the University of Texas at Austin. They were lab partners. My mother thought my father was the most handsome man she'd ever seen, but also quite arrogant. She wanted nothing to do with him."

The audience laughed.

Shanna's mom smiled and her dad shook his head.

"My father was so involved in his classes and attending school that he didn't notice my mom. Something she's never let him forget," Patrick said with a jovial tone.

Shanna's parents laughed.

"Fast forward a few years and they were both at a party. My dad sauntered over to my mom and tried his smoothest line. She didn't give him the time of day." Patrick smiled and nodded.

"Fair play," her mom shouted.

"He decided he wanted to date her, so he found out who she was and where she lived, never realizing she'd been his lab partner."

"I was focused on school at the time," her father said in a loud voice.

"He finally found her at the Kappa Gamma house. He asked her out and she said no. When he asked her why, she told him she didn't want to date anyone who had such a bad memory. He was dumb-founded and left." Patrick held his hand up. "But, the next day, she felt bad, and she found him, with the help of her roommate, at a local burger place near campus. She reminded him that they'd been lab partners and when he asked for her forgiveness, she asked him on a date right then and there. They've been together ever since and are now celebrating thirty years of marriage."

The crowd applauded.

"Mom and Dad, please, have this first dance together." Patrick gestured for them to get up from their chairs.

They stood and walked, hand in hand, out onto the dance floor. The live band began playing a song that Shanna recognized as her parents' song. She couldn't help but smile as she watched them.

"Great story. And look how long it's lasted," Cole said.

Shanna nodded, grateful that her parents were still together. She wanted a marriage that would endure the test of time. She'd thought it would be with Greg, but she'd been wrong. Would she find that same kind of love and commitment that her parents had?

"Not many people make it to thirty years," he said, breaking into her thoughts.

"With all the other crazy stuff in my life, I could always count on my mom and dad loving each other." Shanna watched her parents in each other's arms as they circled the dance floor seemingly lost in their love story.

"I feel that way about my parents too. Always made me feel secure."

Shanna rested her hand across her chest, her throat thick with emotion.

After her parents finished dancing, and the crowd applauded, her brother stepped up to the microphone again. "I, personally, am very glad you got married."

People laughed.

"Happy anniversary. Here's to another thirty years." He clapped and everyone joined in.

"Thank you," Shanna's dad said into the microphone.

Her mom threw her brother a kiss.

"Now, everyone, enjoy the music of The Armadillos," Patrick said. He stepped away from the microphone.

The band began playing a song and Cole leaned over to Shanna, "Let's go show everyone how it's done."

She couldn't resist such an offer. "You love to dance, don't you?"

"With the right partner, yes."

His words made her stomach flip-flop.

He guided her, using his hand on the small of her back, out to the dance floor. She placed her hand in his and warmth emanated up her arm and rushed straight into her chest. He pulled her close to him and her lungs constricted. How could she feel like this after only meeting him yesterday? It didn't matter. Time didn't matter. She was going to enjoy this moment to the fullest.

As they swayed to the music, she lost herself in his strong embrace. Together they were like one fluid movement. When the song ended, she was disappointed, because she wasn't ready to stop feeling his arms around her.

"Let's dance again," he whispered, his warm breath tickling her ear.

She had no problem agreeing to another dance.

They began dancing to a slow song, his hand firmly on her back keeping her close to him. Then he twirled her out away from him. She wasn't very good at these dance steps, but he showed her how to do them. They danced around the floor doing twirls. He pulled her in and dipped her. She came up from the dip laughing. She hadn't had this much fun in a long time. Dancing with him two nights in a row was making her think things she probably shouldn't.

After a few more dances, Cole said, "Let's take a break." He held his hand out for her and she slid hers inside his. He led her over to the table where there was a punch bowl. Grabbing a glass of red punch for each of them, he inclined his head to a door that led outside.

They stood near a railing and Shanna watched the descending sun paint the clouds with pinks and oranges. It was the beginning of a spectacular sunset.

"I'm glad you came," she said.

"I am too." He took a sip of his punch.

"There are so many people here. I'm glad they all came to support my parents. It's nice to see that so many people care about them."

Cole nodded.

"I'd like to have one of these someday." She stepped to the railing and leaned against it.

"An anniversary celebration?" He moved closer to her, making it harder for her to breathe.

"Yeah."

"You want to get married?" he asked, then cleared his throat. "I mean . . . well, you know, like someday . . . to someone." He gulped his punch.

She laughed, then said, "I know what you were trying to say." She paused. "Yeah, I'd like to eventually get married. When the time is right. I'm still trying to get my career going." She didn't want to think about all the work she still had to do for her presentation and another proposal, plus a client meeting. She had so much to do and should be somewhere with her laptop getting ready. But her desire to be here with Cole, celebrating her parents, was even stronger than wanting to work, which was a strange feeling for her.

Lacey came out of the glass door. "Shanna, your mom was wondering where you are."

"Oh." She stood straight. "Does she need me?"

"I don't know. She wanted me to see where you were." Lacey shrugged.

"I'm here." She gave her a cheesy smile.

"Let's go back in and dance," Cole said, extending his hand again. She liked how naturally her hand fit in his.

Inside the room, the band played *Amarillo by Morning*, which made the crowd whoop and holler. Shanna and Cole looked at each other and laughed. They walked out to the dance floor and started dancing. She liked how he held her. Not too tight. Not too loose. Just right.

"George Strait knows how to sing," Cole said.

"Of course, everyone loves this song here."

"My mom loves George," he said. "She went to his concerts."

Shanna laughed. "Was she a groupie? You know, followed him around?"

"I don't think so, but she used to play all his albums. I think I know most of his songs by heart." Cole's smile enveloped his face, making Shanna think he was enjoying himself as much as she was.

They moved easily around the dance floor. Shanna was having a blast—her face was beginning to hurt from smiling so much. This 'enjoying the moment' thing was still new, but definitely appealing.

"When did your parents get married?" She wanted to know more about Cole and his family.

"September of 1982. In the small church by the edge of the river in Juniper Springs, actually."

"Wow." She envisioned the romantic day with Belle wearing a beautiful white gown. She looked at him. "In the eighties, huh?"

"Yep."

"So, you must be pretty old," she teased.

He smiled. "They were married almost ten years before they had me."

The band ended the song and Cole stepped back. For a moment, they were caught in each other's gaze and everyone else seemed to melt away. Shanna's heartbeat thundered in her ears, while Cole slipped a glance at her lips. He peered at her and moved closer. Was he going to kiss her? Right here on the dance floor? In front of everyone? She prepared herself to receive the anticipated kiss.

"Oh, Shanna, there you are," her mom said, breaking the spell.

"Mom." She stepped back and shook her head to gain her composure. "Yes, here I am." *What terrible timing.*

"Look who finally made it," her mom said with a grin. Shanna gazed around her mom's shoulder and there stood Greg, her ex. The one she thought she'd marry. The one who accepted a job in Dallas and basically forgot about her. The one she didn't want to see again.

"Greg?" She blinked, the room around her shrinking.

"Hi, Shann," he said in his oh-so-familiar way.

Jerking her head back, she said, "What are you doing here?"

"Your mom invited me to come celebrate." He smiled, exposing those perfect teeth she'd once admired.

"She did?" It suddenly made sense. Her mom hadn't wanted Cole to be there because she'd invited Greg. And she kept looking around to see if he was there. Shanna wanted to scream.

Almost giddy, her mom said, "Yes, yes. I ran into Emily, and she told me that Greg was going to be in town for a few weeks, so I asked for his contact information and invited him." Her mom acted like it was the best thing that had ever happened.

"I wasn't expecting a text from your mom, of course, but I wanted to come to the party. I would've been here sooner, but I had to go over a file from work," he said, scooping her up into his arms. "It's so good to see you."

Shanna stepped back from Greg, still reeling from the shock. "I think I'd be less surprised to see Taylor Swift standing here."

"Isn't this fantastic?" her mom said with a victorious grin. "The two of you together." She clasped her hands together.

Glancing at Cole, Shanna said to Greg, "I'd like you to meet Cole."

Cole extended his hand. "Nice to meet you."

Gesturing to Shanna, her mom said, "Shanna's car broke down near some podunk town and this young man, nice as he is, towed her car into town. And then even drove her down here so she wouldn't miss the party. Isn't that sweet?" Shanna's mom smiled and patted Cole on the shoulder like he was some sort of errand boy or something. It was so patronizing.

Greg eyed Cole. "Thanks for doing that." As if Cole needed Greg's gratitude for anything.

Cole didn't get ruffled. He gave Greg the same, sincere smile that tugged at Shanna's heart.

"Let's get you something to eat, Greg," her mom said. She

motioned for him to follow her. "We'll be right back. Don't go anywhere, Shanna."

"Yeah, don't go anywhere." Greg winked.

After they left, Shanna said, "That was awkward. I'm sorry."

"Looks like you two need some time to talk," Cole said.

"No." She waved her hand. "The time to talk was years ago." Shanna didn't have anything left to say to Greg.

"He seems—"

"I don't care what he seems. We should dance again." Shanna wanted to forget what just happened and go back to dancing with Cole.

"I think I'd like to get another drink," Cole said.

"I'll go with you," Shanna said.

"You heard your mom." He dipped his head. "Don't worry. I'll be back."

It was obvious Cole wanted to get away from her and she didn't blame him. How could her mom invite Greg and not tell her?

Shanna sat at a table with a whoosh. Her feelings were all jumbled. She was having so much fun with Cole. And that was a problem because she'd probably never see him again. It was silly to feel anything about him.

And now, there was Greg. She was over him. That was for sure. Shanna had spent way too much time waiting for him. Waiting for him to call. Waiting for him to come visit. Waiting for him to take the next step. She wasn't interested in that again. Maybe he was only there to celebrate her parents, and this didn't have anything to do with her. Maybe she was getting ahead of herself.

Lacey sat next to her.

"Did you know my mom invited Greg?" Shanna asked, massaging her temples.

With raised eyebrows, Lacey said, "Nope. She never said a word about it."

"She never talks about him?" Shanna quizzed Lacey.

Lacey paused for a moment before she said, "I didn't say that."

Shanna blew out a breath. "What does she say?" Shanna had no idea that her mom had been talking about Greg. That ship had sailed long, long ago.

Lacey looked around. "That she wishes the two of you would get back together and get married."

"Is that all?"

"No. That the two of you are a perfect match and she's never liked anyone else that you dated." Lacey gave her a sympathetic look.

"Great." Shanna rested her head in her hands. No wonder she'd acted weird around Cole. Except there was no reason to do that because Cole wasn't her boyfriend or anything.

"She talks to his mom every now and then about the two of you, too."

Shanna gazed at her sister-in-law. "Awesome."

"And now he's here." Lacey pasted on a smile.

"Yes," she nodded, "now he's here."

"Was it crazy to see him?" Lacey peered at her with compassion in her eyes.

"Absolutely. No idea he'd be here. Not a clue." She felt like she'd been sideswiped by a bus.

Lacey set her hand on Shanna's. "How are you feeling?"

Glancing at the ceiling, then back to Lacey, Shanna said, "I was head over heels for him. I couldn't imagine my future without him in it." She tapped the table with her fingers. "But that was a long time ago. He kept leading me along with promises that he'd make a more serious commitment when the time was right. Finally, I was done waiting." She was sure she'd made the right decision to end things with him. Wasn't she?

"And now there's Cole," Lacey said softly.

Shanna shook her head. "He has nothing to do with any of this."

"You're sure?" Lacey asked.

"Yes. I'm sure." But she wasn't. Meeting Cole had made an unexpected impact on her heart.

From behind them, her mom said, "You can sit here by Shanna."

Greg sat next to her, and Shanna drew in a breath. He was still as handsome as she remembered with his deep brown eyes and chiseled features. The physical attraction had never been a problem. But relationships were much more than that. Shanna needed a man who made the effort to be with her and left her without any doubt that he wanted her to be his.

Her mom beamed as if she'd solved world hunger. "Isn't this nice?"

Shanna gave her mom a taut smile.

"How have you been, Shann?" Greg said, using his pet name for her.

"Good. You?" She wasn't that interested in his answer. She was far more interested in locating Cole. Where was he? She hoped that snake, Amelia, wasn't talking to him.

"Shann?" Greg said with eagerness.

"Yeah?" She tried to focus on him but kept scanning the room for Cole.

"You seem distracted or something," he said.

"I'm in shock. I didn't expect, to, well, you know, see you. Not here. Not ever." That was the truth. Since he lived in Dallas and she lived in Denver, she figured their paths wouldn't cross.

"Of course, we were going to see each other again." He said it as if it was common knowledge.

"Of course? What does that mean?" Was he going to come find her in Denver at some point? Or they'd meet randomly somewhere else?

He leaned in close enough that she caught a whiff of his familiar musky cologne. "We belong together. Nothing else is more important."

"Really?" She studied him. What she would have given to hear these words two years ago.

"Yes." He said it like he believed it.

"This isn't the time or place to even talk about this." She was concerned Cole had left. She didn't want him to leave before she could explain to him that Greg wasn't part of her life anymore. Did that matter? Did Cole care? She hoped so because she felt there was a connection between them.

"Because you have that driver guy here?" Greg said it so flippantly, as if Cole didn't matter.

She adjusted her weight in her seat, her heart beating erratically. "That *driver guy* has been nothing but kind and helpful," she said, trying to keep her emotions under control.

"Sounds boring." He shrugged and slipped a bit of mashed potatoes into his mouth.

Shanna stood. She didn't want to sit next to Greg and listen to him bad-mouth Cole, someone he knew nothing about. Maybe she didn't know a lot about Cole, but she knew enough. He was a good guy who went out of his way to make sure she could attend this event. Greg had never done something like that for her.

"Where are you going?" Greg asked, surprise etched on his face.

"I need to find—"

"Come on, sit back down. Let's talk. I promise to listen." He patted the chair.

Emphasizing her words, Shanna said, "You aren't even listening right now. I said this is not the place."

"When can we talk then?" He wore a penitent expression. Was he sincere?

Emotions churned in Shanna's stomach. "I don't know."

She turned and started walking. Scanning the room for Cole, Shanna didn't see him anywhere. Finally, after another circle around the room, she went outside and there he was sitting in a chair.

"Hey," she said as she walked up. "I'm so sorry about—"

"Please, stop apologizing. You haven't done anything wrong." He crossed his ankles and gazed out across a pond with a fountain in the middle.

She pulled a metal chair next to him and sat, then laid her head back so she could gaze at the night sky. The warm almost-summer air wrapped around her.

For several minutes, they sat and said nothing. She appreciated that Cole didn't push her to say anything. He simply let her be so she could try to make sense of her rambling thoughts.

Finally, she said, "We'd been together for a long time, but things never progressed past dating. We never moved on to the next step." She'd spent so much time waiting and hoping.

"And you wanted to?" Cole said.

"Yeah. I wanted to get married. I thought he was my forever person, but I got tired of waiting and waiting. I've moved on." She had moved on, hadn't she?

"Maybe he's here to fix things?" Cole tapped his hand on the arm of the chair.

Shanna didn't say anything. It was hard for her to put her feelings into words. Silly as it was, she had feelings for Cole. She enjoyed talking to him, laughing with him, and being in his arms, but she knew they weren't a good match. There were too many obstacles. Besides, Cole needed a woman who was vastly different from her.

"You should take all the time you need to figure things out," Cole said quietly.

Shanna let out a long breath.

"I appreciate you inviting me to this party. It's been nice to meet your family and the food was delicious. I've enjoyed it," Cole said.

"I hear a *but* coming." Shanna braced for it.

Leaning forward in his chair, he said, "It's probably best for me to hit the road." He set his hands on his knees.

"You'll be on the road so late." She wanted to convince him to stay.

"It's fine." He nodded. "I've driven late at night before."

"You can stay." She didn't want him to leave yet because she wasn't ready for this, whatever *this* was, to be over.

Cole stood and Shanna followed suit.

They'd been having a lovely time until Greg showed up. Taking a chance, she laid her hand on his arm. "Please, don't feel like you need to leave."

"I need to get back and help my mom," he said, casting his gaze to the floor.

Shanna swallowed the disappointment that rose up in her throat. "What about my car?"

"Jimmy Bob should be in touch."

She nodded. She'd hoped Cole would take her back with him tomorrow so they could spend more time together, but she didn't

113

dare ask now. Cole's body language communicated very clearly that he was anxious to leave her, and she couldn't blame him.

"Thank you again for all you've done," she said. What else could she say? *I think I might have feelings for you.* She'd sound like a crazy person.

Cole gave a small wave, then left.

CHAPTER 14

Cole started his truck. He pulled out onto the road, second guessing himself. Finally, he convinced himself this was the best course of action. There was no sense in him staying. He'd wanted to offer to bring her back with him so she could get her car, but after seeing her with her old boyfriend, he realized that this whole thing wasn't going to go anywhere.

What did he expect? Did he think she was going to fall for him? In a few days?

He shook his head, then let out a laugh.

It was true that he found her attractive. He enjoyed talking to her. Her laugh and the way she bit her lip when she was thinking was endearing. He felt comfortable with her—comfortable enough that he'd shared some things he hadn't shared with anyone else.

He wasn't sure why he felt so at ease with a woman he'd hardly knew. He absolutely didn't believe in love at first sight, but there was something about Shanna.

It didn't matter though. He was on his way home, and he would probably never see her again. He planned to make himself scarce on Monday when he assumed she'd be back in town. He also assumed Greg would be the one bringing her because there was still something between them—at least that's what it seemed like. He wanted to skip all of that. He'd been there, done that with Deidre and with Melissa. He wasn't interested in repeating it for a third time. Besides, his responsibility was to help his mom get back on her feet and that's what he needed to focus on, not a woman who passed through town with a boyfriend on her heels.

He cycled through some radio stations until he found one he liked. It would be a long drive home that would allow him to clear his head. And he needed that.

After he drove for thirty minutes or so, "Should've Been a Cowboy" came on and his thoughts shot back to trying to teach Shanna to line dance at the Moonlit Bar. She really struggled to follow the steps—his shin could attest to that. He smiled to himself and let the thoughts linger before he pushed them out.

Someday, he might—emphasis on *might*—be interested in a relationship, but not now.

CHAPTER 15

Shanna sat at the table nursing a cup of punch. She let a long breath escape her lips while she reflected on the evening. *What a disaster.*

"Where did Cole go?" Lacey asked as she sat in the chair next to Shanna.

"He left." She drummed her fingers on the table, hoping the party was about over and she could go back to the house.

"Left where?" Lacey crinkled her nose.

"Back to Juniper Springs." She envisioned him sitting in the cab, his strong hands on the wheel while he drove through the darkness away from her.

"Now?" Lacey said.

"Yeah," she answered, feeling deflated.

"Why did he leave?"

"I don't know. Maybe seeing Greg." It had turned into a weird night once Greg had arrived.

Lacey leaned back in her chair. "That's too bad."

She looked at her sister-in-law. "Maybe, but it's for the best." It actually was. She'd let her mind run around in all sorts of directions and entertain thoughts of things that were never going to happen with Cole. It was good for her to face the truth, even if it left a gap in her heart.

"Are you going to talk to Greg?" Lacey waved at Patrick, who gave her a grin from across the room.

"I don't know. I feel like a pretzel." That was the best way to describe it.

Lacey laughed. "I'm sorry. I know this isn't funny, but that visual."

Shanna nodded, trying to find humor in it, but there was nothing comical about the way she felt.

Greg made his way to the table and Lacey left. "Look," he said, "I know this is a surprise. I didn't mean to blindside you." He sat in the chair Lacey had occupied.

"I know." She believed him. Her mother had orchestrated all of this.

He scooted closer to her. "I've missed you. I've missed *us*."

She didn't say anything because she was so confused by the whole evening.

"Can we talk?" Greg asked. He sounded sincere.

After considering his request, Shanna said, "You know, I'm exhausted. I don't think I could do much talking right now." She hadn't felt this drained in a long time, even after pulling all-nighters for work.

He rested his hand on hers. "Tomorrow? Can I come get you at your parents'?"

"Let me think about it." She needed some time to process everything.

"Look at you two," her mom said as she approached. "You should dance."

Shanna gave her mom a pasted-on smile. She didn't want to damper the evening, but she was annoyed that her mom would invite Greg and not even tell her. And she was irritated that it made Cole leave, as irrational as that sounded.

"Would you like to dance?' Greg asked.

"I don't think so. Thank you, though." Shanna couldn't imagine trying to dance right now.

"Greg, is that you?" came a voice that made Shanna want to jump out of her skin.

"Hi, Amelia," he said.

"I thought it was you." She smiled and Shanna wished her teeth would all fall out.

"Maybe we could dance?" Amelia said.

Greg looked at Shanna, who nodded her approval, although Greg didn't need to ask permission from Shanna to dance with Amelia. This seemed a lot like what happened in high school, but Shanna didn't feel the same way about it. Except for the part where she still didn't like Amelia.

She was grateful to Amelia because this provided a much-needed break for Shanna. She got up and searched for her brother.

"There you are," Shanna said when she found him by the snack table.

"Having fun?" He gave her his familiar grin, complete with the crooked incisor because he refused to wear his retainer when they were teenagers.

Knowing she could be honest with Patrick, she answered, "Not really."

"Why?" He faced her.

"Did Lacey tell you that Mom invited Greg?" She tried to sound less irritated than she was.

"No. I hadn't heard that." He peered at her. "I've been busy checking on things."

"Yep. He's here." She fanned her hand out toward the dance floor.

"How do you feel about that?" Patrick asked.

"Tired," she said.

Her brother laughed. "Not what I expected you to say. You were so in love with him."

"I was. But he wouldn't ever commit." Maybe he had changed.

"And now?"

"I'm not sure." Her world felt topsy-turvy.

"What about . . . Cole?" Patrick asked, keeping his gaze on Shanna.

Shanna tensed. "What about him? I don't have feelings for him, you know. I only met him this weekend. You can't have feelings for someone that fast. I mean, sure, he's really great, and good-looking, but what do I really know about him? Except that I like being around him. And talking to him, but that doesn't mean I have feelings for him. Pshaw." She adjusted her stance.

"I meant, what about him, like where is he?" Patrick said, tilting his head.

"Oh. . . Uh . . ." Shanna swiped at her warm cheeks, then cleared her throat. "He left. He's driving back to Colorado."

"I see." The way he said it held much more meaning than the simple words.

Placing a hand on her hip, Shanna said, "What?"

"Nothing. Sheesh, you are so defensive. Or something." Patrick moved an empty bowl off the snack table.

Changing the subject. Shanna asked, "Can you give me a ride home?"

"I would but I have to finish up here. The party isn't over yet and Lacey wants me to make sure everything gets cleaned up afterward," he said.

"All right." She'd have to make other arrangements if she wanted to go home now.

As they were talking, Greg walked up to them.

"Enjoy your dance?" Shanna said. Her tone was sharper than she intended.

"Hey, Shann, there's nothing between her and me. You knew that back in high school. And it's the same now," Greg said, extending his hand out toward her.

Shanna bit her lip. "I'm sorry. I'm overly tired and need to go home, but I don't have a car." Thanks to Greg, she was rideless.

"I'm happy to take you."

She stiffened. "I'm not sure that'd be a good idea."

"I promise, no talking." He crossed his heart.

Shanna thought about it for a few moments. She was being too sensitive. Once she got more sleep, she'd feel better and put everything in its proper perspective. She'd get her car back, go home to

120

Denver, and put this weekend behind her, including meeting Cole. She nodded and said, "Thanks. Can we go now?"

"You'd better say goodbye to Mom," Patrick said.

Shanna gazed around the room before she spotted her mom who was engaged in a conversation with two other women. Shanna walked up to her.

"Hi, Mom."

"Oh, Shanna, dear. Meet Susan and Miranda." She gestured to a tall woman with long, blond hair and to a woman wearing glasses and a black dress.

"Hi." Shanna waved to the unfamiliar women.

The women both acknowledged her, and then her mom said to them, "Can you excuse us for a moment?"

The women nodded, then walked away.

"What's going on, Shanna?" her mom asked with a concerned expression.

"Nothing serious. I wanted to say goodbye."

"You're leaving. Already?" her mom said.

Shanna nodded. "I'm really tired."

Her mom reached out and caressed her cheek. "I'm so happy you came. This party has been lovely."

"That was all Patrick and Lacey." She didn't want to take any credit because she hadn't done anything for the party.

"It's been a wonderful celebration." Her mom's eye glistened.

Shanna hugged her mom, then said, "I'll see you at home."

"We should be home in a while. Your father is making his rounds talking to people. I'm happy to see so many old friends." She peered at Shanna. "How are you getting home?"

"Greg said he'd take me." Shanna said it flatly, hoping her mom wouldn't read more into it.

"Oh." A smile splashed across her mom's face.

Shanna shook her head and left.

CHAPTER 16

On the way home, in Greg's luxurious, silver Lexus, he said, "It's great to be back in town."

"Do you miss Amarillo?" Shanna asked, wondering if he ever thought of life before Dallas.

"I do." He smiled and glanced at her.

"Are you enjoying living in Dallas?" Shanna had been to Dallas a couple of times when she was younger, but she wasn't very familiar with it.

"I am. Dallas is a fantastic city. There are so many opportunities. I'm happy every day that I took this job." It was obvious he loved his life.

Shanna gazed out the window, feeling a pang of something. It was because he'd taken a job in Dallas, and she'd taken a job in Denver, that they'd broken up.

"And you like Denver?" he asked, seeming to be interested in her answer.

"Yeah. Colorado has mountains and a lot of snow. The people—it's definitely a different vibe from Amarillo." She couldn't quite put it into words.

He gave her a sideways glance. "You ever think about moving?"

There it was. He'd been priming her to ask this question. Without beating around the bush, she said, "You mean to Dallas, for example."

Greg shrugged.

"You said we weren't going to talk about us." Shanna didn't want to discuss anything about them right now. She was too exhausted from everything, and her mind felt like mush.

"I know." He waved his hand. "I'm sorry. It's just that I've dated a lot of women."

"Okay." What was the point of telling her that? So he could rub it in?

He cleared his throat. "I mean, I've dated a lot of women and none of them compared to you."

She blinked, unsure what to say.

"I was really happy when your mom invited me so I could have an excuse to see you again."

She closed her eyes, then twirled a piece of her hair around her finger while she considered his words. Drawing in a deep breath, then letting it out slowly, she said, "This came out of nowhere for me." She hadn't heard from Greg since they'd broken up.

Nodding, he said, "I realize that."

"Can we stop talking about it for now?" All sorts of thoughts bounced around her head and ran into each other, making her feel dizzy.

"Will you promise me to think about us?" he asked.

"I don't know, Greg." She wasn't willing to make any promises.

"Well, I'll be over tomorrow and maybe we can talk then?"

"Maybe." She didn't want to commit to anything. Greg had led her on for years and she wasn't about to jump back into anything with him.

He glanced at her. "Can we go to breakfast?"

"I'd like to spend breakfast with my parents." She didn't want to give up time with her mom and dad to spend it with Greg.

"Afterwards?" He seemed accommodating, which was different than the Greg she'd known.

"How about if I text you?" Shanna needed time to settle her

thoughts and get her bearings. She'd never expected the man she'd once loved and wanted to marry would come crashing back into her life.

"All right."

Greg seemed so eager to talk to her. She wished he'd been that eager years ago to talk and make a solid commitment. They'd be in a different place right now. But he hadn't. And they weren't.

They drove the rest of the way in silence listening to the music on the radio. When they got to the house, Greg turned to her and said, "I've never stopped loving you."

"I'll text you tomorrow." With that, Shanna got out of the car and went inside.

CHAPTER 17

Shanna took the stairs slowly as she made her way to her room. All her feelings were twisted into knots and double knots—maybe even triple knots. Being in her old bedroom was kind of messing with her anyway. Every time she came home, she felt a little off balance, like she'd been swallowed in a portal that sent her back ten years. Was she an adult who had a life in Denver or was she still a teenager simply imagining it?

She decided to take a warm shower. As the water cascaded down her back, her thoughts went to Greg. There was a time she would've walked on hot coals for him. She'd loved him so much and planned on a beautiful life together. But she'd finally realized he wasn't ready to settle down and she didn't know if he ever would be. They'd drifted apart and she focused all her energy on her life in Denver. A life that didn't include Greg. She thought that was the end of it.

And then her car broke down. Spending time in Juniper Springs with the people there had touched her heart in a way she didn't expect. The warm greeting and the way they made her feel like she was family was so natural. And Cole? Well, he'd made an impression the second she saw him exit that oversized tow truck wearing his cowboy hat. She'd been immediately attracted. But it was more than his handsome features. They seemed to connect quickly. She felt safe with him, not only physically, but emotionally as well. As if she could tell him anything and he'd listen. That was something Greg had rarely done.

But a relationship with Cole was out of the question. As soon as he left the party, she knew that. They lived in different worlds, and nothing was going to change that. Even if he were interested in pursuing something, it was doomed before it even started. Long-distance relationships didn't work. Period. She'd learned that lesson well from Greg.

Still, the idea of being with Cole circled her mind. The way his arms felt around her. The way he smelled of spearmint and the outdoors. The way he'd treated her as if he was eager to hear what she said and how she felt. And the way she'd yearned to kiss him. *Oh, that.* If they hadn't been interrupted, she would have pressed her lips to his and savored every moment.

Several more minutes passed while the bathroom steamed up from the hot water. Finally, Shanna decided to shut the water off and get out.

Wearing her silk pajamas she'd bought from Nordstrom's in Denver, she snuggled into her old bed.

A knock sounded. She wasn't in the mood to speak to anyone, but when it sounded again, she said, "Who is it?"

"Mom."

Shanna sat up in bed. "Come in."

Her mom walked into the bedroom. "Wow, you got comfy pretty fast."

"I needed a nice hot shower to help me relax."

"Because you have things to think about?" she said, then sat on the bed.

"Yes." Shanna smoothed the white comforter.

Trying to suppress a smile, her mom said, "Because you're thinking about Greg?"

Shanna didn't say anything.

"I knew it." She clasped her hands together. "I knew if I could get the two of you in the same room together again, you'd both realize that you should be a couple."

Shanna interlaced her fingers and rested them on her lap. She was irritated that her mom had invited Greg without telling her, but she didn't want to get into a big discussion about it, so she swallowed the words that wanted to escape her lips.

Her mom reached out and rested her hand on Shanna's. "I'm sorry I didn't tell you. I wanted it to be a surprise."

"Which is why you were so weird when Cole drove me here."

Her mom nodded. "He seems to be a nice young man, but Greg, well, he is your one true love."

"Greg didn't want to commit." Shanna had already explained this to her mom.

"But time has passed, and I think he's ready," she said earnestly, then rubbed Shanna's arm.

Shanna jerked her head back, her pulse increasing. "Wait. You talked to him?"

She waved her hand. "Of course not."

After a couple of moments, realization dawned on Shanna. "Oh, you talked to his mom."

"It doesn't matter." She peered at Shanna. "What matters is that the two of you get your second chance."

Shanna didn't want to talk about it anymore. "Did you enjoy the party?" she asked, changing the subject.

"Yes. It was wonderful." Her mom beamed.

"You and Dad looked happy." Shanna was grateful her parents still enjoyed each other.

Pointing a finger in the air, her mom said, "That man drives me crazy sometimes, but I love him, and I always will."

Shanna reached over and gave her mom a hug despite her irritation with her mom's shenanigans. After all, her mom meant well.

"I'll let you get some sleep." Her mom stood and left.

Shanna burrowed under her covers. Tomorrow was a new day and things would look different. At least she hoped they would.

CHAPTER 18

Cole walked into the kitchen of the inn. "Hi, Mom."

"Good morning." She poured him a glass of orange juice. "You weren't in the house this morning when I got up. I assumed you were still in Texas."

"No. I was out taking care of one of the cows that got stuck in a fence." He sipped his juice.

She opened the refrigerator door and put the juice away. "Oh, those cows. Always getting into trouble," she said, shutting the door. "Your dad sure loved having cattle."

Cole nodded, feeling the emptiness of losing his dad.

His mom gazed at him. "You seem troubled."

"Missing Dad, I guess." He didn't think he'd ever get used to his dad's absence.

His mom reached over and caressed his shoulder. "How was the drive to Texas?"

"Fine." He grabbed one of the freshly baked blueberry muffins.

Leaning against the counter, his mom asked, "And the party you went to. Was it nice?"

"Yeah." Scenes of holding Shanna in his arms flashed through his mind.

She studied him.

He shifted his weight. "Do we have people checking out soon?" He needed to focus on something so his brain didn't get mired in memories.

"Son, don't change the subject." She placed her hand on her hip. "Tell me about Shanna."

"Nothing to tell." He gulped the rest of his orange juice, then set the glass in the sink. "I was going to work on the plumbing in the bathroom today."

"Seems like something happened," she said, not letting the subject go.

"Nothing happened, Mom, really." What could he say? *I wanted to kiss her but then her ex made his grand entrance.* It was better to forget about the whole thing.

"Good morning," Madi said brightly. "Hey, Cole. How did things go with Shanna?"

"I think something happened," his mom said.

"Like what?" Madi asked, grabbing a muffin.

"He won't say," his mom said.

"You know, I'm right here in the room with you. You're talking like I'm not here." Cole didn't want to have this conversation and he especially didn't want his mom and cousin to have it, either. His love life, or lack of one, was no one's business but his, and he didn't want to talk about it.

"Well, if you'd say something we wouldn't have to," his mom said, pointing at him.

"You look like Eeyore from Winnie the Pooh," Madi said.

"Seriously?" He didn't look like that pathetic donkey, and he wished they'd leave him alone.

"Yeah. You don't look very happy." Madi bit into her muffin.

Trying to keep his voice even, he said, "Let me explain this. I towed a woman's car to the garage. She needed a ride to an event—"

"That was four hours away," Madi said, cutting in.

Cole gave her a look. "And I drove her. Now I'm home." It was pretty cut and dry. There was no need to discuss it further.

"But we want to know what happened at the party," Madi said. She was getting on his nerves, but he knew she wasn't going to let up until he gave her something.

"We ate dinner," he said.

"And?" his mom asked expectantly. Between his mom and his cousin, he was outnumbered.

"We danced," he said, giving in.

Madi nodded with a toothy grin.

"And then?" his mom said with wide eyes.

"Then her old boyfriend showed up and I came home." Anger and disappointment shot through him at the recollection.

"Ohhhh. Now it's clear," his mom said.

"Yep, he was jealous," Madi sang out.

"Jealous?" he said, his voice louder than he meant.

"Because you really like her." Madi laughed.

"I need to get to the plumbing. I'll see you two later." Cole left and went upstairs to the bathroom. Working with plumbing wasn't his favorite, but it was far more preferable to talking to his mom and Madi.

He took his tools and removed the P-trap to see if it was clogged. It was. He cleaned it out and replaced it.

For the record, he wasn't jealous. Why would he be jealous? Sure, he liked Shanna. She was a nice person. Sure, they had a good time dancing. But when her old boyfriend, whatever his name was, showed up it was time for him to go home. He knew that. And it was fine. He didn't need any complications from a woman, no matter how much he enjoyed being around her. Life was simpler on his own.

He made a mental note to stay away from the garage tomorrow.

CHAPTER 19

Shanna awoke to the light streaming into her bedroom. As a teen, she'd hated the sunlight coming in and waking her up, but as an adult she appreciated the sunshine alerting her to a new day so she could get more done. She dressed and went downstairs for breakfast.

"Good morning, Shanna Bug," her dad said, putting down his cup of coffee.

"Hi, Dad." She sat in the chair next to him. "Did you enjoy the party last night?"

"I did." He sipped his coffee. "It couldn't have been better."

"Patrick and Lacey did a great job," Shanna said, reaching for a toasted bagel.

"Your mom was really happy, and I was able to talk to a lot of people I haven't seen in eons." He bit into his bagel and smudged some cream cheese on his face.

Shanna smiled, then handed her dad a napkin and pointed to the spot on his face. "I'm glad it went well."

After he put the napkin down, he said, "I saw Greg."

"He was there."

"Your mom thinks the two of you are getting back together." He studied her, making her fidget.

"I think she's way ahead of herself." Shanna wished her mom would stay out of it.

"You'll know what to do." He gave her a nod, then patted her hand. She was grateful that her dad trusted her to figure out her own life, something her mom had a hard time accepting.

"Good morning," her mom said as she entered the kitchen. "It's a beautiful day."

Shanna agreed.

"I'm going to go to church this morning. Would either of you like to join me?" her mom asked.

"I'd love to go," her dad said.

Her mom turned to her. "Shanna?"

"Let me check on a few things. I need to figure out how to get to Denver tomorrow." She needed time to do some last-minute prep for her presentation on Tuesday. She was regretting that she'd spent the weekend playing and dancing instead of working. Her focus needed to be on her job and nothing else.

"What options do you have?" her dad asked.

"I don't know exactly. I was thinking about flying." She hadn't considered all her alternatives yet.

"Why do you have to be there tomorrow?"

"I have an important presentation for a new client on Tuesday that's been scheduled for a month. I'm not quite ready for it. I'm supposed to have a meeting tomorrow afternoon with a coworker who's been working on the print aspect."

"I'm sure your boss would understand," her mom said as she sat at the table.

Shanna held up her hand. "No, no. My boss would not understand."

Shanna's phone buzzed. "Hello?"

"Hi, this is Jimmy Bob. You know, Jimmy Bob from the garage where your car is."

How could she forget? "Hi, Jimmy Bob."

"I wanted to tell you that I got confirmation the water pump is on the way. I'll be able to fix your car and it'll be ready for you tomorrow afternoon," he said with a cheery tone.

"Thank you so much." She appreciated Jimmy Bob's efforts to keep her updated and hoped he was as good at repairing her car as he was at customer service.

"I'll see you tomorrow."

She said goodbye and ended the call.

"News about your car?" her dad asked, his attention on her.

"Yeah, Jimmy Bob said it'll be ready tomorrow afternoon." Hopefully, he was right.

"Jimmy Bob?" her mom said with an arched eyebrow.

"Yeah, he's the mechanic." Shanna liked Jimmy Bob.

"You're on a first-name basis with the mechanic?" her mom said, sounding alarmed.

Feeling defensive, Shanna said, "Yes, Mom. He's a super nice guy and he's rushing the repairs for me."

"How will you pick it up?" her dad asked.

"Hmm. Good question. I'm not sure yet. I'll be in Denver, but I'll have to get back to Juniper Springs, somehow. Maybe pick it up on Tuesday." She hadn't settled on her plans to get her car. Her first order of business was to get back in time to prepare everything for the presentation.

"Maybe they have a bus," her dad said.

"No, they don't. I checked on that when my car broke down. It's okay, I'll figure it out." Shanna was a big girl and she'd make it work.

They finished eating breakfast and Shanna went up to her room. She turned her computer on and there was a message from her boss.

"Send me the final images. ASAP." Shanna stared at it.

She hadn't finished the social media campaign. There were a couple more images she needed to edit for Twitter and another one for Instagram. With everything that had been going on, she hadn't had time to spend on the presentation. If she had any hope of making it shine, she had to buckle down and get those final images to Renae as quickly as possible.

After an hour or so of editing eye-catching images and adding compelling text, her phone buzzed with a text. It was from Greg.

Can I come over now?

I'm working, she texted back.

When is a good time? She could feel the impatience from his words.

Not sure. She couldn't think about anything but getting these images back to her boss.

Her phone rang. Greg's name popped up on her screen. Seeing his name on her screen used to make her heartbeat speed up but it didn't have the same effect now. "Hi, Greg," she said as evenly as she could.

"Please let me come over," he insisted.

Closing her eyes for a moment, she said, "I need to put the final touches on my presentation."

"I won't take a lot of your time. Please?" He sounded serious.

"All right. Come over in an hour." She could give him a few minutes to say what he needed to say.

"See you then."

After spending most of the next hour going over everything for Renae, she dressed in a simple green skirt and white blouse.

A few minutes later, the doorbell rang, and she went downstairs to answer it since she was the only one home. She opened the door to Greg.

He was as handsome as ever with his deep brown eyes and wavy brown hair. He was wearing navy blue dress pants and a blue and white striped polo. "Hi," he said.

"Come in." She opened the door wider.

Greg walked past her and into the living room. "The house hasn't changed much," he said, gazing around.

"Mom did a kitchen renovation last year but nothing out here." Maybe the change wasn't readily apparent, but it was still there.

"You look beautiful." He smiled at her in the same way he did for so many years.

"Thank you." She motioned for him to sit on the cream-colored, oversized couch.

Greg sat and Shanna followed, sitting on the loveseat across from him.

"Can you come sit by me?" He patted the seat cushion.

"Sure." She sat next to him and could smell his musky cologne, which sent her mind tumbling back to a time and place when they were together and in love.

"I don't know how to start, so I'll jump in," Greg said.

She peered at him.

"I know I took you for granted." He held his hand in front of him. "I got so caught up in my career that I didn't give much thought to what was going on between us. I didn't give us the same kind of attention I gave to my job." He seemed contrite.

She nodded. How she wished he'd said this years ago.

"You tried to tell me, but I didn't want to hear you." He placed his hand on hers. "You were right to break it off, because once you did, it made me stop and think."

"That was almost two years ago," Shanna said, trying to be unaffected by what he was saying.

"Well, I'm a slow thinker." He laughed.

Shanna gave him a tight smile.

"Since then, I've realized how amazing you are and how much I miss us together. When I think of my future, I see you in it."

He was laying it all out there for her, but she wasn't sure what to do with *it*. She'd never expected Greg to be at her parents' party, let alone say all of this. She'd put her lingering feelings to rest over a year ago.

"I'm hoping you'd be willing to give me another chance and let me show you that I still love you," he said earnestly.

His words sounded nice. Better than nice. But, as he'd proven so many times in the past, his words were empty. Hollow. And now, without the emotional attachment she'd once had, the words didn't hold much weight.

"I know I screwed up. I know this was my fault. Please, will you consider giving us another chance?" He gazed at her with pleading in his eyes. "What we had was so good."

"It was good. . . Until it wasn't," she said with a firmness she hadn't ever used with him.

"I know. I let you down. But I've learned from that, and I think we can make something great out of this again." He seemed to be sincere. Maybe he had changed, and things would be different. Maybe . . .

"But you live in Dallas, and I live in Denver. Long-distance relationships don't work." Even if she were interested in giving him another chance, they had already proven that distance was too much of a hurdle for them.

"I thought about that." He raised his finger in the air and wore a proud expression.

"You did?" She watched him, wondering what he was going to say next.

With enthusiasm, he said, "Yeah. I have a friend who works at Hardwick Public Relations, and I've been talking to him about you. They're very interested in interviewing you." He gave her a wide grin as if he'd solved all the world's problems. Or at least hers.

"They are?" He'd talked to someone about hiring her? Was this being sweet or something else? A nagging feeling settled in her gut.

"Yes. And I think you'd love living in Dallas." He was almost boisterous.

"I would?" He hadn't even asked how she felt about any of this.

"Absolutely!" He grasped her hands in his.

"But I love living in Denver." She'd made a place there for herself.

He nodded. "I know, but Dallas would offer you more opportunities, believe me."

She stood and walked to the other side of the sofa. Turning back to him, she said, "So you're proposing that I move to Dallas, and we get back together?" Shanna wanted to make sure she understood.

"Yes, exactly." He grinned, then stood. "Yes."

She made her way back over to him. "What about you moving to Denver?"

He blinked a few times as if he hadn't comprehended what she said. "Oh, well, I'm poised to move up in the company and I don't want to jeopardize that."

"I see." She sat on the couch again, trying to take in all he was saying.

Sitting next to her, he put his arm around her shoulders. "This is all for us. It'd be so good."

Shanna gazed out the window at the Cedar Elm tree she used to play under when she was a girl. She wasn't sure what to think or how to feel. Two years ago, she'd have given anything to hear him say these same words. But he hadn't. And Shanna had moved on. At least she'd thought so.

Greg pulled her toward him. "Tell me you'll give us another chance."

"I don't know what to say, Greg. This . . . I don't even know." She stood again and went to the window.

"I should've reached out sooner," he said.

"Yeah, you should have." She twirled a piece of her hair around her finger while her mind ran in circles.

He stood and walked over to her. "But tell me we still have a chance."

Holding him at arm's length, she said, "I need time to think."

"Of course. Take all the time you need." He held his hands up.

"I need that time to think *alone*." She couldn't think straight with him hovering over her.

"Oh, yeah. Of course." He backed away from her. "I can go now."

"That'd be a good idea," she said.

"Can I call you later?"

"I don't know." She had to be honest. She wasn't sure about what he'd said or how she felt or what any of it meant. Her brain felt like a puzzle with several pieces missing.

"Whatever you say, Shann. I just want us to be together. We were really good together, weren't we?" He looked at her, his eyes urging her to answer in the affirmative.

Shanna bit her lip, then gave a slight nod. It was true that they were good together. At one time. In the past. She walked Greg to the door.

"Thank you for letting me come over. I'll wait to hear from you," he said.

She gave him a noncommittal shrug.

After he left, she shut the door and stood there with her forehead against it. Of all the things she thought would happen, the sun falling out of the sky was more likely than Greg coming to see her and admitting he was wrong. He'd never done that before. Telling her he wanted her back were words she'd ached to hear for a year after she broke up with him. But those words never came. Until today.

"Was that Greg I heard?" her dad said, startling her out of her thoughts. "Sorry, I didn't mean to scare you. I just got home and saw an unfamiliar car in the driveway."

"It's okay. Yeah, it was Greg." She let out a long breath. "Where's Mom?"

"I dropped her off at Patrick's to watch the boys for a bit."

Shanna nodded.

Her dad walked into the living room, and she followed him.

"What did Greg want?" He sat in the leather chair by the fireplace.

"To get back together," Shanna said, sitting in the other leather chair, her head still spinning.

"Smart boy. You are quite a catch." He gave her his best dad smile.

"Thanks, Daddy." Her dad was her best cheerleader. He'd worked long hours while she was growing up and then spent time serving as mayor, so she didn't see him as much as she would've liked, but he never missed an opportunity to tell her he loved her and thought she could change the world. Of course, he'd made it clear he believed that part of the world was in Amarillo, but he still supported her career move to Denver. Her mom, not so much.

"What did you tell him?" Her father kept his gaze on her.

"That I needed to think about it." It was the only thing she could say.

"Well, how do you feel?" He leaned forward in his chair.

"Confused." She rubbed her temples. "As you know, we were together for a long time. I wanted to get married, but he was content with the way things were, so I broke it off. He said that made him realize that he'd taken me for granted. So now he wants me to move to Dallas so we can be together."

"Is that what you want?" he asked.

She didn't have an answer.

"You should take all the time you need to figure it out. I want you to be happy," her dad said. "If Greg is the one who will make you happy, then I'm all for it."

"Mom, obviously, wants us back together. She orchestrated the whole thing last night." Irritation pricked her.

"She shouldn't have meddled in it." A disapproving expression crossed his face. "If I'd known, I would have told her that."

"It took me by surprise." She twisted her hair tightly around her forefinger. "It's not the only thing that's taken me by surprise this weekend," she said softly.

Her dad perked up. "What do you mean?"

She shrugged a shoulder.

"Are you talking about the young man who drove you here?" He gave her a quizzical look.

She argued with herself if she should say anything to her dad. Finally, she said, "Maybe."

He raised his eyebrows. "He made quite an impression on you."

"It's hard to explain." She laid her head back and closed her eyes. After a minute or so, she opened her eyes. "We've only known each other for a few days, but somehow, I feel this connection to him. It goes against all common sense, I know. You can't fall for someone at first glance. It takes a long time to get to know someone." She felt foolish even saying it out loud.

"Perhaps," he said in a nebulous tone.

Shanna looked at her dad. "It took a long time for you and Mom to get together."

"I was an idiot." He waved his hand.

"That's what she says, too," Shanna said with a wide grin.

He laughed. "I should have dated her right when we met."

"Why didn't you?" She'd never asked her dad this question.

"Simple, really. I was too focused on myself and getting through school." He crossed his ankles.

"Good thing you ended up together." If they hadn't, Shanna and Patrick wouldn't be here, which was a sobering thought.

"Best decision I ever made," he said, giving his leg a sturdy pat to emphasize his words.

"See," she held her hands out toward her father, "I want what you and Mom have."

"You can." He nodded.

"I'm not sure I can with Greg. He took me for granted and it wasn't until I left that he realized he wanted me. I don't want that. I want a man who realizes he wants me when he's with me. A man who thinks being with me is the best decision he's ever made." Things were becoming clearer to her.

"And you think . . . Cole might be like that?"

She cast her gaze to her hands, her fingers intertwined, "I don't know. I just felt something unexplainable and undeniable for him." It sounded a little insane that she felt strongly about a man she barely knew. She wasn't some Disney princess who fell in love at the ball. She was an intelligent, thoughtful woman who prided herself on her common sense. And this went against all common sense.

Leaning on his elbow, he asked, "What are you going to do about it?"

"Nothing." She blew out a breath of defeat.

"Nothing?" His voice rose an octave.

She straightened in her chair and tucked her foot under her other leg. "I don't know what I can do. He left." The moment when he said goodbye flashed through her mind and left a pit of sadness in her stomach.

"Because of Greg?"

"I think so." It was the only explanation. Up until Greg barged in, they were having an amazing time dancing and talking. She didn't want the night to end.

"But you do have to get your car. Maybe you can see him then. You could talk to him," her dad offered.

"I think it'll be too uncomfortable to see him now." She couldn't even imagine the awkwardness.

"Maybe not."

She cradled her head in her hands. "I don't know what to do. I need to be in Denver. And I need to somehow get my car." She collapsed back against the chair.

"How can I help you?" her dad said with sincerity.

"I don't know. I think I'll go up and rest for a bit and try to figure things out." Maybe if she took a little time to relax, things would sort themselves out and she'd know precisely what to do.

CHAPTER 20

Shanna sat on her bed, staring at nothing in particular when her phone rang, jerking her out of her stupor. "Hello?"

"Hey, how has your weekend been?" Kaylie said.

"Where to even begin? It's been the craziest weekend," Shanna said.

"How so?" Kaylie asked.

"My car broke down about three hours after I left." It was only two days ago, but it felt like it had been months ago.

"Oh, no." Kaylie's voice carried a sympathetic tone.

"I had to have it towed and I ended up in this tiny, little town." A tiny, little, quaint, wonderful town.

"Are you still there?" Kaylie said. "Did you miss your parents' anniversary party?"

"No. I left my car there to get it fixed. It needs a water pump. I'm in Amarillo."

"How did you get there?"

Stifling a smile, Shanna said calmly, "The guy who towed my car gave me a ride."

"Well, that's a full-service towing company." She laughed. "Talk about customer satisfaction. Right?"

Shanna didn't want to go into all the details at the moment. "He was very nice to bring me here. But now I'm without a car and I need to finish the presentation and meet with Christine tomorrow because she's doing the print campaign."

"What are you going to do?" Kaylie asked.

"Try to book a flight." She hoped there'd be one available tonight back to Denver. She'd have to worry about her car later.

"What do you need me to do?" Kaylie said.

"Make sure we have all the materials ready to show Christine. I'll send you the newest images." With Kaylie's help, Shanna could pull this off. Probably. But she desperately needed to find a flight back.

"Will do," Kaylie said. "How will you get your car?"

"I'm still working on that." Shanna was sure she'd figure something out. Maybe after her presentation, she'd find a way to get to Juniper Springs.

"I'll see you in the morning, Shanna."

"See you then. Thanks, Kaylie."

Shanna was grateful for her assistant. Kaylie was dependable and reliable as well as a good friend.

Picking up her laptop, Shanna started searching for flights. Every airline she checked was full. There weren't any seats on any flight at all. What was she going to do?

A knock sounded at her door. "Come in."

"Hi, hon."

"Hey, Mom." Shanna kept searching through all the available flights, hoping a reservation would suddenly become available.

Her mom sat on the bed beside her. "What are you doing?"

"Trying to find a flight back to Denver, but everything seems to be full." Shanna was trying to stay calm and not freak out.

"Oh, good. You can stay another day," she said with a giddy expression.

"No, I can't. I need to get back home." Her mom didn't understand the urgency.

"You are *home*," her mom said with emphasis.

"To Denver." Shanna didn't want to hurt her mom's feelings, but Amarillo wasn't her home anymore.

143

"Maybe this is a sign." She rubbed Shanna's back.

"I'm going to start looking for a rental car." Shanna began searching through sites to see what cars were available.

"Tell me all about Greg," her mom said.

Shanna continued to scroll through car rentals. She was sure one would be available, even though it was so last minute.

"Well?" her mom said with an expectant tone.

"He wants to get back together." She tried to keep her voice even.

Her mom clapped. "Oh, I was hoping you'd say that. You and Greg are such a perfect couple."

"I told him I'd have to think about it." She wanted to be clear with her mom, so she didn't start calling wedding planners.

"What's there to think about? You love Greg. You always have. And he loves you. Perfect. We could do a Christmas wedding if we get on it right away."

Shanna looked directly at her mom. "I'm not very happy that you ambushed me, first off, but second, you're getting way ahead of yourself." She needed to rein in her mom.

"I'm excited for you." Her mom's eyes were practically dancing.

Drawing in a breath of courage, Shanna said, "I'm not sure I want to get back together with Greg." She knew her mom wouldn't like this answer, but she deserved to know that there wasn't an imminent wedding.

"What reason could you possibly have?" She drew her brows together. "He's perfect for you."

She wanted to give it to her mom straight, but in the easiest possible way. Yes, she was irritated that her mom thrust Greg's surprise visit on her, especially when Shanna was enjoying the evening with Cole, but she knew her mom meant well, even if it came across as meddling. Her mom wanted Greg and Shanna back together—that much was obvious —but this was her life and she needed to be upfront. "I understand that you think Greg and I belong together, but I'm not sure *my* heart is in it."

She patted Shanna's hand. "If you give it some time, I'm sure you'll realize that it's the right thing to do."

Realizing that her mom wasn't going to relent when it came to Greg, Shanna said, "For now, I need to find a way back to Denver."

A knock sounded. "This is the popular place to be, I guess," Shanna said. "Come in."

Her dad walked into her bedroom. "I have a great idea."

"You do?" she asked.

"I checked my schedule, and I can drive you tomorrow."

"To Denver? That's a long drive." Shanna didn't want to impose on her dad, and they'd have to leave early in the morning for her to make her afternoon meeting.

"What if I drive you to get your car in that small town? You'll have your car to drive back to Denver," he said. "Problem solved."

Not wanting to rain on his parade, she hesitated to mention her meeting and instead said, "That's a wonderful offer."

"We can leave in the morning." He smiled with pride.

"I'd love to go, too," her mom said, "but I have a meeting with my accountant in the morning and I can't move it."

"Road trip with the two of us then," her dad said, rubbing his hands together.

Shanna smiled, but her stomach twisted because she wouldn't be able to meet her coworker. She'd have to try to change the meeting to Tuesday morning and hope Christine would agree.

"It'll be nice for you and your father to have some time together," her mom said.

Shanna nodded. Her mom was right. This would be a great opportunity to enjoy the moment with her dad. Cole would approve—if that mattered. Which it didn't.

"Since you'll be home tonight, I can call and invite Greg over. I'm sure he's—"

"Mom, please. Let's have a simple dinner together. I'm not really in the mood to entertain Greg or anyone else. And I need to get some work done." Now it was crunch time since she'd be arriving home later than she'd anticipated. Who was she kidding? This whole weekend had been different than she anticipated.

"But it'd be so nice to have Greg over. Like old times," her mom said.

"It isn't *old times* anymore." Shanna wanted to make that clear. "I really need to get some work done on my presentation for Tuesday."

"We'll let you get to it then," her dad said. He held out his hand to her mom and they both left the room.

~

SHANNA CAME DOWNSTAIRS FOR DINNER. She could hear giggling which could only mean one thing.

"Aunt Shanna," said Griffin.

"Hi." She outstretched her arms and he rushed in for a hug. "Wow, Grif, you are so much taller than the last time I saw you."

"Mom says it's because I eat my vegetables. They make me grow." He stood on his tiptoes.

"Actually," said Spencer, "it's because you're a human and humans grow at this age."

"Come here and give me a hug, Spencie," Shanna said to her oldest nephew.

Spencer rolled his eyes, then gave her a hug.

"Sorry, I didn't mean to call you by that nickname." Shanna swiped at her mouth, then mimicked throwing something away. "Won't happen again.

"I am eight now, Aunt Shanna. Too old for nicknames," he said matter-of-factly.

Shanna laughed. "It's so good to see you two. I've missed you."

"You should come visit more," Griffin said with wide brown eyes.

"I agree," her brother said.

"Make that unanimous." Lacey gave her a hug.

"Let's all sit down for dinner," her mom said. "I've made some shrimp fettuccine."

"Mmm, smells delicious," Patrick said.

They sat around the table. Shanna couldn't help but smile. Though she enjoyed her life in Denver, she'd missed her family and having dinner together.

"What's the deal with your car?" Patrick asked, then shoveled in some fettuccine.

"It should be ready tomorrow. Dad has volunteered to drive me to Juniper Springs." Shanna sipped some water.

"Will you see Cole?" Lacey asked.

Shanna shrugged. "I don't know." She wasn't sure what would happen.

"Pass the rolls, please," Spencer said. "Grandma makes the best rolls."

Shanna's mom beamed. "Why, thank you."

After dinner, Lacey and Shanna sat on the loveseat by the big window overlooking the yard. The boys ran out and started swinging.

"It's great to see the boys. They sure grow fast," Shanna said.

"That they do. I have to keep buying them new clothes almost every month." Lacey laughed. "So, tell me about what's going on."

Shanna gazed up at the ceiling. "Well, Greg came over earlier."

"Oh. How was that?"

"He wants to get back together."

Lacey studied her. "Do you?"

"I'm not sure. I mean, he said all the right things. Things I'd wanted to hear two years ago." She ran her fingers through her hair.

"Better late than never?" Lacey said, encouragement in her eyes.

"I don't know. I have a life in Denver. And . . ." she didn't finish her sentence.

"And?" Lacey raised her eyebrows.

Shanna wasn't sure how to put her feelings into words. The things Greg had said tempted her to give him another chance, but the way she felt with and around Cole gave her pause.

"Is this about Cole?"

Shanna's cheeks warmed. "It sounds foolish."

"What?" Lacey prodded.

"That I could have any feelings for him." Love at first sight wasn't actually a thing and Shanna was silly to even think it.

Lacy patted Shanna's arm, then laughed. "You know my story. As soon as I met Patrick, that was it. I fell fast and hard."

"You just knew?" Shanna had never been so interested in Lacey and Patrick's love story.

"I didn't know I wanted to marry him necessarily, but I definitely knew I wanted to date him the moment I met him." Lacey held up her hands.

"I know that Greg and I make a great team. We have chemistry, or at least we did. He's a good guy, but I wouldn't want to be taken for granted again." That was her real fear—she'd become involved with Greg again only to repeat history.

"And Cole?"

"He has this warmth about him. He's so kind. And he makes me feel something inside I haven't felt in a long time. But we're so different. And there's the whole distance thing."

"Just because long distance didn't work with Greg doesn't mean it can't work with Cole," Lacey said.

"What if he doesn't feel the same way?" Shanna realized that she'd buried herself in work since her breakup with Greg to avoid risking her heart again. Meeting Cole had made her reconsider.

"You won't know unless you see him."

"I don't know."

Lacey peered at Shanna. "Your heart will tell you what to do."

"Anyone want some dessert? It's strawberry cheesecake," her mom said as she entered the room.

"Hmm, I can't say no to that," Lacey said with a laugh.

"Same." Shanna loved her mom's cheesecake.

AFTER DESSERT AND MORE VISITING, Shanna gave her brother, sister-in-law, and her two adorable nephews big hugs and promised to keep in touch better.

"Let's FaceTime, Aunt Shanna," Spencer said.

148

"You got it. I promise we will." Shanna waved to them as they drove off. She walked back inside.

"About what time do you want to leave in the morning?" her dad asked.

"I need to do a conference call, but after that. Maybe by nine o'clock." Shanna had called Christine and left a message about rescheduling the meeting, so the only thing she had to do was this conference call.

"That will get us there early afternoon," he said.

"Yeah, I think my car should be ready by then." She was depending on Jimmy Bob to have it done as he said he would.

CHAPTER 21

*a*fter her conference call Monday morning, Shanna started gathering her things. She was grateful she'd been able to reschedule the meeting with Christine to tomorrow morning. Maybe things were beginning to work out on this trip. *Finally*.

A knock sounded.

"Shanna," came her mom's voice

"Yes?" she said as she packed up the last of her stuff.

"You have a visitor," her mom said.

She stopped packing and looked toward the still closed door. "Who?"

Silence.

"Mom?" she said, her heart rate beginning to speed up.

Still silence.

Shanna went to the door and opened it. "Is it Greg?" she said.

The look on her mom's face confirmed it.

Tamping down her irritation, she said, "Mom, I told you not to get involved."

"I didn't. I had nothing to do with this." She shrugged.

Shanna wasn't sure she believed her mom since she'd been plotting to get them together all weekend.

150

"He's here to see you." She gestured toward the stairs.

Drawing in a deep breath, Shanna said, "You love this."

"I'd love to see the two of you back together."

"Tell him I'm not here." Shanna didn't want to talk to Greg or see him. It would only confuse her more.

"Shanna, go talk to him," her mom said with firmness. "He came over to see you and the polite thing to do is to talk to him."

"Fine." Shanna walked down the stairs trying to control the tug of war going on inside her. This weekend had left her feeling dazed.

"Hi, Shann," he said when she approached the entryway.

"Hi, Greg." She said it as evenly as possible.

"I know you said to give you some time, but I didn't want to go back to Dallas without seeing you." He peered at her.

Shanna nodded, unsure of how to respond to the man who suddenly popped back into her life with declarations of love.

"I want you to know that I mean what I said. I know I made mistakes and I'm sorry. I've learned from them, and I want to make this work between us." He stepped toward her.

Backing away from him, she said, "I don't know what to say."

He held his hand up. "You don't have to say anything."

They stood there for a few awkward moments. Greg said, "I'm glad I came this weekend. It was so good to see you."

"It was good to see you." She meant it. Even though she hadn't expected to see him or expected him to say what he did, it was still good to see him. No matter what, they shared a history and she'd loved him deeply. Once. Maybe she still did. She wasn't sure.

"Can I call you?" he asked, then moved toward the front door.

"I don't know." Was she ready to give him another chance? To take a risk on someone who hadn't fought for their relationship? Someone who hadn't made her a priority?

"I'll leave it in your hands then. I hope to hear from you soon," he said with the same smile she'd loved for so many years. He opened the door and walked outside.

She nodded, then followed him out the door and onto the porch.

As he made his way to his car, she said, "Travel safe, Greg."

He turned and said, "You, too."

He got in his car and drove out of the driveway. She watched him turn down the street, then she came back into the house.

"So?" her mom said, clasping her hands together and smiling like the Chesire Cat.

"Sweetheart, stop suffocating the girl. Let her decide what she wants to do," her dad said.

"But—"

"Really, Mom. I know you want us together. But I don't know if that will happen." She didn't want to disappoint her mom, but she couldn't fall into a relationship with Greg simply to please her. Shanna didn't want to get involved with Greg unless she was sure she'd have no regrets.

"I'll try to stay out of it." Her mom glanced at her watch. "Oh, I've got to go. Please, drive safe. And come home again soon!" She gave Shanna a tight embrace.

"Bye, Mom. It was a great party. I'm glad I came." Even with Greg's surprise visit and her mom's well-intentioned interference, Shanna was glad she'd come to the party to celebrate her parents.

"I'm so glad you came too." Her mom caressed Shanna's cheek. "I love you."

"I love you, too," Shanna said.

Her parents kissed, then her mom turned and left.

"I can get your stuff and put it in the car," her dad said with a smile.

"Thanks, Daddy."

SHANNA and her dad drove away from the house in a brand-new charcoal gray Ford Explorer. One of the perks of owning a car dealership was that her parents always drove the newest models.

Once they were on the road, she said, "Thank you so much for taking time away from everything to drive me." She knew her dad was busy running his successful business and preparing to run for another political office.

"No worries, Shanna Bug." He reached over and patted her hand.

She was too old for his nickname. "Dad."

"I've missed you. I wish you didn't live so far away. What does Denver have that Amarillo doesn't? I'm sure I could get you a job here." It wasn't the first time he'd offered.

"*That* is what Denver has."

"What does that mean?" He scrunched his nose as if she'd spoken in a foreign language.

She wanted her dad to understand what she meant. "Dad, you were the mayor. You own one of the biggest dealerships in the area. Mom owns a business. Everyone knows me as your daughter. That's how they see me. I wanted to be my own person. I wanted to go where no one knew Shanna *Lyndley*."

He blinked. "Is that such a bad thing?"

"No, of course not. But I wanted to be independent. Make my own decisions. Make my own mistakes." She wanted him to understand that she was trying to find her own identity and be her own person on her own terms.

"And you have?" he asked.

"Made mistakes? Sure, plenty of them." She laughed.

He shook his head. "That's not what I meant."

"Yes, I've made a life for myself in Denver." What she had in Denver she had because of what *she'd* done. She didn't have to worry that she was only successful because of her parents.

Her dad seemed to consider her words. After a few minutes, he said, "I guess I can see where you're coming from. I'm very proud of your success in Denver. You've done well for yourself up there."

She smiled. "Thank you."

He glanced at her. "I do wish you were closer so we could see you more often. We all miss you."

"I miss you, too." Shanna missed her family, but she was thankful she'd made the decision to go to Denver and make her own way.

Her phone rang. "Hello?"

"Uh, hi, yes, this is Jimmy Bob. Jimmy Bob at Davis Car Repair. The one who has your Honda," he said.

"Yes, Jimmy Bob, I know who you are," she said with a smile.

"I wanted to tell you that I got the water pump and I'm, uh, working on your car now." Shanna could practically see Jimmy Bob's face as he said this.

"Thank you."

"It should be ready for you in a few hours," he said.

"Perfect. I'm a few hours away."

By the time she got to Juniper Springs, her car would be done, and she could drive back home to Denver. A part of her hoped to see Cole, but another part of her—the sensible part—hoped she wouldn't see him. Meeting him had complicated things and seeing him again would only complicate them further. Greg's proposal that they get back together swam around her mind and she needed to think things through without notions of Cole getting in the way.

CHAPTER 22

*W*hen Cole walked into the lobby of the inn, his mom asked, "Can you run some errands for me?"

"Sure, Mom. What do you need?" He liked being at her disposal. He couldn't change the fact that his dad had passed, but he could make the transition as easy as possible for his mother.

"I have a list." She handed him a piece of paper. "And the fence fell over behind the shed. Would you mind putting it back up?"

"I'll get right on it." Cole looked over the list, then folded the paper and shoved it into his pocket.

Wearing a blue bandana on her head and carrying a bucket of cleaning supplies while walking down the stairs, Madi said, "Aunt Belle, I finished cleaning the River Room."

Memories of Shanna shot through Cole's mind at the mention of the River Room.

"Thank you," his mom said. "We have some guests arriving in about an hour."

Cole collected some nails and a hammer and set out to fix the fence. While he was out there, he tried to focus on the job, but his thoughts kept going back to Shanna. For whatever reason, he felt connected to her. If her ex hadn't shown up at the party, he would've kept dancing with her and—what did it matter? He had shown up and Cole had already done this rodeo—twice—and he wasn't about to do it again. Better that the ex came and Cole made a quick exit before he gave another woman a chance to trample on his heart.

"Cole?" came Madi's voice.

"Yeah?" He stopped pounding nails into the post and faced his cousin.

"The dishwasher is leaking water all over the floor. Can you help?" She frantically gestured toward the inn.

Cole jogged back to the inn and rushed inside. Sure enough, the floor looked like a pond.

"I turned it on like I always do," Madi said. "I don't know what happened."

"It's not your fault," his mom said. "It's been needing to be replaced for quite a while." She handed Cole a towel.

Cole tossed the towel on the floor to soak up the water, then turned the supply line off to the dishwasher.

"Good thing you were here," Madi said. "I don't know what we'd do if you weren't." She was on her hands and knees wiping up the water.

"I'm glad I was here too." It was these experiences that made him want to move back to Juniper Springs so he could be here full time to help.

His mom pointed at him. "Now, don't be thinking you're indispensable. I can certainly call Benji Jones to come do some handyman jobs." She gave him a curt nod.

"You said you hated how he fixed stuff," Madi said with a crinkled nose.

"Oh, hush. It'll be fine." His mom gave Madi a sharp look.

"Mom?" It was time to have a serious conversation.

"Never mind her. I don't want you to feel obligated to keep staying here. You have a career to go back to." She picked up a soggy towel.

Cole studied his mom. It was true that he had a practice to return to in Fort Collins, but it was obvious she needed him here, even if she was acting like she didn't. "I've been meaning to tell you."

"What?" She eyed him.

"I've been thinking that I'll be staying for a while." He'd been considering his options. While he liked Fort Collins, the truth was it was too big for him. He wasn't much for living in the city. With his mom needing his help at the inn, the garage, and the ranch, it just made sense for him to come back.

"A while?" his mom said.

"What does that mean?" Madi gazed at him.

"Indefinitely." He didn't want to make a permanent decision, but he figured he would probably stay in Juniper Springs.

"What about the law practice?" His mom set the dripping towel in the sink.

"I can do some work remotely." He paused for a moment to collect his thoughts before saying them out loud. "But I'm actually thinking about opening my own office."

"Here? In Juniper Springs?" His mom jerked her head back.

"Yeah."

"Oh, that'd be wonderful," his mom said, then threw her arms around his neck. After she stepped back, she said, "But only if that's what you really want to do."

"I need to make a trip to Fort Collins and get my stuff from my apartment. Tie up some loose ends." Moving back to Juniper Springs was feeling more and more like the right thing to do.

"But, honey, are you sure you want to come back to Juniper Springs?" His mom studied him like he was the Mona Lisa.

"Yeah, I think I do." He reached over for another towel and mopped up some more water.

A bell rang out in the lobby.

"I'll go," Madi said. She dropped her wet towel in the sink.

"Cole, I don't want you to put your life on hold for me. I can get along, you know." His mom straightened.

"I know you can. But I've realized that Fort Collins isn't the place for *me*. I like life here better." It was true that moving back to help his mom was his first priority, but Juniper Springs was a better fit for him as well.

"That makes me so happy." She reached over and hugged him again. "Now, I need to attend to some things. Thank you for helping with the dishwasher."

"You're welcome," he said with a smile.

His mom left and Cole finished securing the dishwasher, then made his way back outside to finish the fence at the furthest corner of the yard by the white shed. While he stood there in the bright sunlight, he felt good. This was the right decision for him. His life wasn't in Fort Collins. It was in Juniper Springs.

After about twenty minutes of work, he was startled by a voice.

"Cole! Cole!" Madi shouted as she ran toward him waving her arms. "I need to tell you something."

"What is it?" His heartbeat sped up as he watched her, hoping it wasn't an emergency. Was his mom all right? Could a guest be hurt?

"I've been trying to call you," she said out of breath.

"I think I left my phone back at the inn. What's going on?" He was trying not to panic.

"It's Jimmy Bob." She took a deep breath, then continued. "He had to leave the garage to go to the hospital."

"Is he okay?" He hoped Jimmy Bob hadn't had an accident or something.

"Yeah, yeah. It's Lizzie. She's having the baby." Madi grinned. "Isn't that awesome?"

"Today? Right now?" He was still in a bit of a shock.

"Jimmy Bob called the front desk and said he was headed to the hospital, and he needed someone to finish work at the garage."

"All right." Cole hadn't done much mechanic work over the last few years, but he could cover for Jimmy Bob. "I'll go right over and see what needs to be done."

CHAPTER 23

Shanna's dad glanced at her and said, "You've been pretty quiet on this drive,"

"I've been thinking." She'd been trying to make sense of her feelings.

"About Greg?" he asked.

"Yeah." She twisted a piece of her hair.

"You think you want to get back together?" He adjusted his grip on the steering wheel.

"He made a lot of points worth considering. We are good together. At least we were." They'd been together for a long time and at the beginning it was wonderful.

"But you weren't happy during the year before you broke it off."

Her dad was right. She'd been pretty miserable. Greg said he'd changed and things would be different this time, but she wasn't sure she believed him. Was she willing to take a risk and end up in the same place as before—waiting for the next step and feeling like she was second-best to his career? "I know. And . . ." How could she put it into words?

"What?" He glanced over at her again.

"I don't know." She let out a long breath, arguing with herself if she should even say anything out loud.

"The young man who drove you home?" her dad said, seeming to sense her thoughts.

She massaged her forehead. "I can't stop thinking about him. I mean, there's no possibility of us getting together. It's just . . . I feel something. I can't even explain it."

"What do you want to do about it?"

"I don't think there is anything I *can* do about it." Why did she feel so connected to a man she hardly knew? What she did know about him, was how different they were. It all seemed so silly to entertain any ideas of her and Cole together.

"Then you've made the decision," her dad said as if it was the easiest decision ever.

She needed to elaborate so her dad could understand her quandary. "But meeting him has thrown me for a loop. Spending that time with him. It was . . . amazing. It's so easy to talk to him. It felt natural. Like there were no worries and no barriers between us. I didn't even think about my job." Being with Cole made Shanna immerse herself in the moment.

"Well, then maybe that's your decision," he said as he shrugged.

"Daddy, you aren't helping." She laid her head back against the seat.

"No one can decide for you, Shanna Bug. Your heart has to make the choice."

She needed to realize that this weekend would be a cherished memory and nothing else. "Well, there isn't really a choice when it comes to Cole."

"Why not?" he held his hand out to Shanna.

Maybe saying it out loud would cement it in her mind. "Because we happened to meet and share a great weekend. Nothing more," she said as convincingly as possible.

"Do you want it to be more?" her dad asked.

She chewed on her lip as she gazed out the window.

"What about Greg?"

Looking at her dad, she said, "I loved him for a long time. He was my one and only. I thought we'd get married. Maybe have a baby by now." The life she thought she'd have flashed before her.

"You could still build a life with him if you want to." He patted her hand.

"I don't think I do. I don't think he's my person." Saying it aloud made her realize it was true. Seeing Greg and hearing him make the declarations she'd wanted to hear had confused her. But now she could see it clearly.

"See, you've made a decision." He smiled at her.

"I guess I have." She didn't know her future, but she did know that Greg was her past and she planned to tell him that when she returned to Denver. "Thanks, Daddy, for talking to me about it."

He nodded, then squeezed her hand.

They drove for thirty minutes without saying anything.

"When we get to this town—" he started.

"Juniper Springs." Saying the name made her heart twitter.

"Yes, when we get there, where do you want to go?" He adjusted his position in his seat.

"To the garage to see about my car." She hoped Jimmy Bob would have it done by the time they got there.

"You know—"

"Don't say it." She held her hand up. "Please."

"But a Ford would—"

"Daddy." She gave him a don't-start-on-me-for-buying-a-Honda look.

"All right." He shrugged.

They pulled into town and Shanna directed her dad over to Davis Car Repair.

"Looks like a nice place," her dad said. "If you have to break down because you aren't driving a Ford."

Shanna rolled her eyes, then got out of the car and walked into the garage. "Hello?"

"Back here," came Jimmy Bob's muffled voice.

Shanna walked behind the desk and over to where her car was

propped up. Jimmy Bob's back was to her, and he was obscured by a large tool chest.

"How's my car?"

Jimmy Bob seemed to freeze for a moment. He turned and Shanna's breath caught. It wasn't Jimmy Bob. It was Cole.

CHAPTER 24

*A*s soon as Cole heard her voice, his heart seized for a moment. She was here. He knew when he got to the garage and saw her car that he'd be working on it. He had hoped to finish it before she got back to Juniper Springs. It wasn't that he didn't want to see her again—he did—but he wasn't willing to get involved with a woman who was involved with another man.

Despite the connection he felt to her, it was better to not even start anything than to risk his heart again.

"Cole?" she said.

He nodded.

"I expected to see Jimmy Bob. He called me and . . ." she said, seeming confused.

"He's at the hospital with his wife," he said simply.

"Oh?"

Feeling like he should add the most important detail, he said, "She's having the baby."

"That's wonderful. I'm so happy for Jimmy Bob," she said, her face lighting up and her eyes sparkling.

Cole cleared his throat, trying to ignore the effect Shanna had on him. "So that left me to finish up your car. I know you're anxious to get on the road." He wanted to help her get back to Denver because he knew she had an important presentation tomorrow.

"I am."

He wanted to ask about the party, but he didn't. He assumed that she spent time with her ex and that they were probably back together. No need to make things awkward.

"Cole," Mr. Lyndley said as he walked into the garage.

"Hello."

"I didn't realize you were a mechanic." He gazed around the garage.

Cole shrugged. "I used to help my dad in the garage when I was a teenager. I haven't worked on cars for a while." He quickly added, "But I've put in enough water pumps to remember how to do it."

"Will Shanna's car be ready soon?" he asked.

"Yes, sir. I need another thirty minutes or so."

"How about some lunch, Shanna Bug?" her father said.

Shanna visibly cringed. "Dad."

Shanna Bug. Cole smiled to himself.

"Sorry about that." Her dad smiled, then turned to Cole. "Any spots you'd recommend for lunch?"

"We can go to Ada's Cafe," Shanna said. "Delicious food and great service. I had a delicious meal there." She glanced at Cole with her bright blue eyes, and he sucked in a breath.

"I'd recommend Ada's," Cole said, reminding himself that there was nothing between them and that scooping her up in his arms was completely out of the question.

"Ada's it is then," her dad said. "You're sure her car will be fixed today?"

"Yes, sir, it will." Cole wanted to reassure them both.

"I need to get back to Amarillo as soon as I can." Her dad gave a nod.

"Thank you, Cole," Shanna said. "You came to my rescue. Again." She smiled and it tugged at Cole's heart.

"We like to make our customers happy. I'll let you know when it's ready." He was trying to keep the conversation professional.

"Thanks. We'll be over at Ada's," she said with a lilt to her voice.

He watched her and her dad walk out of the shop, then gave himself a swat on the forehead. He couldn't deny that he was physically attracted to Shanna, but it was more than that. He liked being around her and listening to her talk. He enjoyed her laugh and the way she spun her hair around her finger. Most of all, he felt so comfortable around her—like he could be himself.

It didn't matter, though. She was probably making plans with that stiff-looking guy she'd dated. Besides, he'd only known her for a short while, not nearly long enough to have legitimate feelings. In another hour or so, she'd drive out of his life, and he'd go on with his newly-formed plans to move back to Juniper Springs.

SHANNA LEFT THE GARAGE, her nerves tingling. Seeing Cole unexpectedly had tangled her emotions. She wished things were different.

She walked with her dad over to the diner and went inside.

"Well, look who it is," Ada said warmly. "Welcome back."

Shanna smiled. "This is my dad. We're grabbing some lunch while Cole finishes my car."

Ada nodded. "Welcome to the diner. I heard Lizzie was having the baby today. I'm glad Cole could jump in. He's an excellent mechanic."

"He said it would be done soon." She hoped he was right so she could get back to her regular, settled, know-what-to-expect life.

"Sit here and look at the menu." Ada gestured for them to sit at a table near the door. She handed Shanna and her dad the menu.

While Shanna looked over the menu, memories of eating here with Cole crashed in.

"What do you suggest?" her dad said.

Pulling herself from the memories of Cole, she said, "The Juniper Burger is very good."

"Your mother would jump up and down if I ordered a hamburger. She has me on this bland diet."

"I won't tell if you don't," Shanna said with a grin.

"Deal. Let's order two of those. And plenty of fries," her dad said.

Ada came over to bring them some waters, then took their orders.

As they waited for their meals, Shanna let her mind wander. She was certain she'd made the right decision about Greg. She was pretty sure the right thing to do about Cole was to forget about him and go back to Denver. Somehow, though, that didn't quite sit well with her.

"Cole seems to be a young man with many talents," her dad said, jarring her back to the present.

She coughed, then said, "Yeah, he seems to be able to do a lot of things." Shanna sipped her water.

"Nice guy, too."

Shanna nodded.

"The two of you—" her father started to say but his phone buzzed. "Hello? . . . What? . . . With no notice? . . . Did he say why?. . . Fine, if I leave right now, I can come in when I get back to Amarillo." He ended the call.

"Problem?" Shanna asked.

He shook his head. "Apparently, my sales manager up and quit today. No notice. Nothing. He's left us high and dry."

"I'm sorry, Daddy," Shanna said. "Is there anything I can do?"

"No, no. It's nothing you need to think about. But I will probably need to get my lunch to go so I can get on the road," he said.

"Don't worry about me." She hoped her dad would get everything worked out at the dealership.

When Ada brought their plates, her dad asked for it to go. Ada brought everything back for him in a bag.

"Thank you so much for driving me here," Shanna said.

"I'm glad I could help. I hate to rush off," her dad said.

"My car should be ready soon and I'll be on the road."

They embraced and she waved at her dad as he left.

Shanna ate her hamburger. It was as good as the first one she ate—juicy and flavorful. It was exactly how a hamburger should taste. And the fries were golden with just enough salt. She could get used to eating at Ada's.

Belle walked into the diner. "Oh, Shanna. I didn't know you were here."

Shanna nodded. "Cole is fixing my car."

"Because Jimmy Bob is waiting for the babe to be born." Belle smiled. "Cole is an excellent mechanic."

"So I've heard," Shanna said with an awkward smile.

"If he doesn't get it done, you can stay with us tonight at the inn," Belle said.

"Thanks. Hopefully, I won't need to stay." She glanced at her watch. "It should be done soon."

"Did the anniversary party go well?" Belle asked in a sincere tone.

"Yes. It was a fantastic event," Shanna said. She refused to let visions of being with Cole slide through her mind.

"Hi, Belle, what can I get you?" Ada asked as she grabbed her pad from her apron.

"Oh, yes. Madi would like an extra-large order of fries and a strawberry shake."

Ada laughed. "To be young and able to eat that way."

"Ain't that the truth?" Belle chuckled.

"I'll get those for you right away," Ada said as she walked back toward the kitchen.

Belle sat in the chair at Shanna's table. "I hope you don't mind if I sit here."

"I'd love it." Shanna felt so warm when she was near Belle. It was as if Belle were her long-lost aunt or something.

The bell jingled on the door and Shanna turned to see who it was. Cole stood there with his cowboy hat in his hand looking as handsome as ever in his oil-smudged white t-shirt, blue jeans, and cowboy boots, but Shanna didn't let her gaze linger on him.

Cole walked over to the table. "Hi, Mom. What are you doing here?"

"Getting some fries and a shake for Madi. That girl would eat here all day if I let her." Belle smiled.

He nodded, then turned to Shanna. "Your car is done."

"Oh, thank you." Shanna's happiness was tinged with a bit of disappointment. She shouted inside her head to get herself together and stop thinking about Cole.

"I can bring it over here."

"No need. I'll finish my lunch and pick it up."

"Your regular, Cole?" Ada asked with her hand on her hip.

"Sure. But I need to get back to the garage."

"I'll have it right out," she said.

Shanna blew out a breath hoping to ease the awkwardness she felt. She said, "Thank you so much for fixing my car."

"It wasn't too difficult. I'm glad we could get the water pump here." He didn't make eye contact with her.

"I'll be able to, you know, get on the road."

"Uh, huh," Cole said.

Ada returned to the table with a bag. "Here are the fries and a strawberry shake for Miss Madison. I added some extra strawberries because I know she loves them."

Belle stood. "Thanks, Ada. You're a dear." She stood and turned to Cole. "I'm going back to the inn."

"See you later, Mom."

"I think it's okay to close the garage early today," Belle said.

Cole nodded.

"I hope to see you again *real soon*." Belle reached out and squeezed Shanna's arm.

Shanna smiled to herself at Belle's transparency.

Belle left the diner.

A cloud of discomfort hung over Cole and Shanna. Neither of them said anything. Cole rocked back and forth on his feet next to the table while he waited for his food and Shanna stared at her burger trying to think of something to say. Finally, Ada returned to the table and set Cole's burger down.

"I need that to go," Cole said. "I need to get back to the garage."

"Nonsense. Sit down and enjoy it with this sweet young thing," Ada said, making Shanna's smile widen at Ada's obvious attempt to make them eat together.

Reluctantly, Cole sat at the table across from Shanna. There wasn't any real reason they couldn't eat lunch at the same table.

"This town is full of busybodies," he muttered.

"I heard that," Ada shouted from behind the counter.

"You don't need to eat here if you'd rather not." Shanna wanted to give him an out.

"I wouldn't want to make Greg upset. Did he come with you?" he said without looking directly at her.

Shanna bit her lip. "No, he didn't come with me."

"Meeting you in Denver?" Cole picked up one of his fries but didn't eat it.

"No," Shanna said, understanding Cole's cool demeanor. He was upset about Greg showing up at the party. "Greg told me he wanted to get back together, if you must know." Shanna wanted to be upfront about what happened.

"I didn't ask." Cole slipped a French fry into his mouth.

"All right, then forget I told you," Shanna said.

Cole looked at her and it made her heart fall to her stomach. "Now that you've said it, you need to . . ."

"Give you details?" she said with an arched eyebrow.

"No." He ate another fry.

Shanna took a bite of her burger and juice dribbled down her face. She grabbed a napkin.

Cole smiled for the first time since he'd come into the diner.

"What?" Shanna asked.

"You have some mayo on your nose."

"I do?" Her cheeks flushed. She hated it when she ate her food with her nose instead of her mouth.

"Right there." He pointed.

Shanna swiped at her nose.

"You got it." He smiled, then visibly relaxed. "Tell me more about Greg."

"He asked me to get back with him." She sipped her water to moisten her dry throat.

"And?"

She licked her lips. "Greg was an important part of my life for a long time. But . . ."

Cole watched her.

"He's not my person anymore." Shanna was as sure of that as she was of the fact the sun would rise tomorrow.

Cole nodded, seeming to hold back a smile.

"At first, I was upset that my mom invited him. She's been trying to get us back together for so long. But then I was glad she did. It finally made it crystal clear that there isn't a future for us."

Cole's eyes widened. "For *us*?"

"For Greg and me," Shanna said, considering Cole's response. Did he somehow think there was a future for them—Shanna and Cole?

"Oh, yeah. That makes sense," he said, seeming to recover from his initial reaction.

"Greg is very focused on Greg and pursuing his career, which is great for him. Not so great for me." Shanna wanted a man who would make her feel like she was more important than anything else.

"You feel good about it?"

"I do." Shanna sipped her water. "How are things here in Juniper Springs?" It sounded lame, but she didn't want their conversation to end. Not yet.

"Good. Before I was summoned to the garage, I was working on some plumbing issues at the inn. I still need to go check on the cows in the south field."

"Oh. That sounds . . . interesting." She tossed a fry into her mouth.

He hesitated for a moment as if he were arguing with himself, then said, "If you aren't in a hurry to get back, you're welcome to come if you'd like."

"I've never been around cows." The closest she'd been to a cow was when she went to the state fair with her cousin back when she was a kid.

"And you probably want to leave as soon as possible so you can get back," he said.

"Yeah. I probably should, so I can work on my presentation." Because her presentation was important—more important than spending time with a man who made every part of her feel alive. Yes, leaving him and driving back to Denver made the most sense for a woman who wanted to get a promotion.

"Because your presentation is tomorrow." He nodded. "Yeah, you probably should get home ASAP," he said with an edge to his voice.

She took a bite of her burger. After she swallowed, she blurted out, "But I could, maybe, delay my drive for a little while." This was against her better judgment but something deep inside drove her to throw caution to the wind.

She needed to leave.

She wanted to stay.

"All right." He smiled and it reached all the way up to his eyes. "It shouldn't take too long."

CHAPTER 25

$\mathcal{A}$fter they finished eating, Shanna followed Cole over to his truck all the while reminding herself this was all in vain, because no matter how strongly she felt about him, this would probably be their last time together since they lived in different cities. Although Fort Collins and Denver weren't *that* far apart. So maybe . . .

Inside the truck where Cole's woodsy cologne lingered, Shanna watched as they drove away from the heart of town and took a road to the west. After a couple of miles, he said, "This is where our property starts." He pointed to some fields lined with trees.

"Wow, looks beautiful." The wide-open spaces met the horizon in the distance.

"I find solace out here. This is my happy place."

Shanna glanced over at him. "I can see that."

He smiled, then adjusted his hat.

They pulled out onto a dirt road. Dust billowed behind them as they drove down a road lined with barbed wire fence.

"It's very quiet out here," she said. This was so far removed from the city life she was used to. No traffic. No buildings. No sidewalks. No businesses. Just fields, trees, and a big, blue sky.

"That's what I like most about it. I can hear myself think and I can consider all the great things about life. Peace and tranquility." He nodded.

"There always seems to be commotion in Denver. When I'm at my apartment I can hear sirens pretty regularly. People arguing outside. Dogs barking. Engines roaring." Shanna liked all the energy of the city, but there was a downside to it too—not a lot of serenity.

"Not much of that out here. Well, except for the barking dogs." He laughed.

He stopped the truck. On the other side of the fence was a herd of black cows. Shanna assumed the smaller cows were younger. Cole opened his door and got out, so Shanna followed suit.

Cole pointed to an animal by itself. "I need to check that steer for pink eye."

"Cows get pink eye?" She'd never heard of an animal getting pink eye, though she'd had it herself a few times.

"Yep."

"What do you do for it?" she asked as she stepped up next to him while he examined the imposing animal.

"We have to treat it with antibiotics," he said. "My grandpa used to pour salt in the eye."

"Salt? Like the kind we use on our table?" She shuddered thinking of a poor animal with salt in its eye.

"Yeah." He took his hat off, smoothed his hair, then put his hat back on. "I remember the first time I saw him do it."

"And that works?" She blinked, her eyes suddenly stinging.

"It does, but nowadays we call the vet. And we treat the whole herd. Except . . ."

"What?" Shanna studied him, anxious to hear what he would say.

Cole massaged the back of his neck. "The vet we've used ever since I can remember passed away and we're waiting for a new vet to come to town."

"You can't treat them for pink eye then?" Shanna found herself much more concerned about a herd of cows than she expected.

"There's a vet that's in the next county. I've put in a call to her." Cole nodded.

Feeling relieved, she said, "I hope she can come treat them soon. Pink eye must hurt."

They walked closer to the herd. None of the animals seemed to mind. Cole stepped over to a large one. "How are you doing today, Gary?" He reached over and patted the animal on its neck.

"Gary?" She started laughing.

"Yeah. Gary is a great name for a steer."

"What is that one's name?" She pointed to a cow.

Cole took a stance and shrugged. "Squidward."

"Wait. You named the cows after cartoon characters?" She remembered watching SpongeBob SquarePants when she was a kid.

"Maybe."

"Where's SpongeBob?" She imagined seeing a cow that resembled a sponge wearing brown pants and a red tie.

"Over there." He pointed to a fat one that almost looked square.

Shanna had to laugh. "I never thought you'd name cows."

"Technically, the females are cows. The males are bulls. And the castrated ones are steers," he said.

Shanna made a face. "Castrated ones?"

"We castrate them so they put on more weight and sell for a higher price when we take them to the sale barn in the fall," he said as if everyone knew this information.

"I don't think I want to know how the whole castration thing happens." Too much more information might make her head implode.

He smiled and tipped his head.

Shanna watched him go over to another cow. She wasn't sure if it was a female or a male. They were all cows to her. Cole was so gentle with the animal. "Have you ever thought about being a vet?" she asked.

"I did. A long time ago." He gently stroked the cow.

"You're really good with these cows, er, bulls, I mean, steers." Seeing him with all the animals made her heart quiver.

"I'd much rather work with animals than people." He laughed. "Especially as an attorney."

"Do many attorneys represent animals?" she asked with a smile.

He chuckled, then said, "What I meant is that in my job as an attorney, I think I see the worst of people."

"Are you going to keep practicing law?" she asked. He seemed so at home out here on the ranch, it was hard to imagine him in a courtroom.

"I think I'm going to move back here permanently." He glanced at her.

"Oh." For a moment, she'd considered seeing if there was anything more between them if he lived in Fort Collins and she lived in Denver because it wasn't *too* long distance. But Juniper Springs would definitely be classified as *long* distance from Denver.

He plunged his hands into his pockets. "I'll go back to Fort Collins and take care of my apartment."

"Any chance . . ." she let it trail off.

"What?" He peered at her with his disarming eyes. She'd never want to face him in court because she'd be putty in his hands.

A white dog ran up to them.

"Oh, hey, Ranger." Cole tousled the dog's fur.

"Yours?" she asked, imagining Cole sitting next to the fireplace with his dog at his feet.

"My mom's, but he loves when I'm here." Cole looked around. "I think we're done. I need to check on some fence down there and make sure the patch I made is still holding. It's a bummer when the cows get out, especially our bull."

"Patrick?" she asked remembering the name of the starfish on SpongeBob.

He smiled. "Mr. Krabs."

"That's quite a name for a bull," she said with a smirk.

"He's quite a bull." He laughed. "He likes to charm the ladies. Once when he got out, I chased him all over the county before I caught him." Cole gave a sharp nod.

They started walking across the field. Cole turned around to say something to her. Shanna wasn't watching closely and stumbled over a rock. Cole caught her in his arms before she fell to the ground. For a moment, they stood there, suspended in time, with their gazes interlocked. Her heartbeat sped up while his arms were wrapped around her. "Be careful," he said. "There's uneven ground out here."

"I don't think I'm wearing the best shoes for this," she said, not wanting to move from his grasp.

"I guess I should've told you . . . to wear . . . some boots." He gently set her straight and stepped back.

They made their way to the truck and drove a quarter of a mile. Cole jumped out and examined the fence. Shanna noticed his muscles flex as he moved his hands over the fence patch and lifted some wire. He got back into the truck. "I think that'll do it."

"You have a beautiful place out here." She could almost imagine herself taking long walks along the fence line.

Cole fanned out his hand. "My dad had a lot of plans for it."

Shanna could feel the sense of loss and sorrow for a man she'd never met because she knew Cole missed him so much. "I'm sorry he passed."

"Me too."

"So now you'll take on his plans?" she asked.

Cole gazed ahead. "I do love being out here."

"I can see that." It was obvious Cole belonged in this country air and fields filled with cows. It was part of him.

They drove back to the house, which was painted a light blue with some white shutters and a white wooden fence in front. "We can go inside and get a drink. Mom usually has a fresh pitcher of lemonade made."

Shanna walked inside the house. On the fireplace mantel were some photos. She looked at each one. Pointing to a photo in a silver frame, she said, "When was this one taken?"

Cole walked over to her. "I think I was five or six. That was my first horse, Patches."

"Such a big smile. And that's your dad?" Happiness oozed from the picture.

"Yeah. He used to take me with him to ride the fences." Cole gestured to the kitchen. "We can get some lemonade in here."

She followed him to the kitchen which looked like a picture out of a magazine. The yellow and white curtains all matched the tablecloth. It felt so homey and inviting. Exactly how she would've imagined a country kitchen.

Cole grabbed the pitcher out of the older-model refrigerator.

Shanna held her glass out and he poured some lemonade. Life here seemed so easy. So calm and natural.

Her phone buzzed. She glanced at it. "It's a text from Kaylie. My assistant," she said, resenting the intrusion.

Cole nodded, then blew out a breath.

Shanna read the text, then pocketed her phone.

"Nothing urgent?" Cole asked, his eyes curious.

"It can wait." How could she explain that being here in Juniper Springs with him had made her think differently about her life? That she felt inexplicably drawn to him? What could she possibly say? *Hello, I know we only met a few days ago, but all I can think about is spending time with you.* It sounded crazy. Possibly even creepy. Yet something inside her had clicked.

The big question remained. Could she do anything about it?

CHAPTER 26

*C*ole drove them back to the garage, trying to tamp down the thoughts that buzzed through his brain. "Here we are," he said as he parked his truck.

"Thank you for taking me out to your house. I enjoyed it," Shanna said.

"Your car shouldn't give you any more problems. But if it does, you have my number."

"Do I?"

"Maybe not. I can put it into your phone. You know, in case you have car problems." He sounded like an idiot.

"Yeah. Of course."

She handed him her phone and he put in his contact information. He gave it back to her and their fingers brushed against each other. He wanted to take her in his arms and kiss her, but he resisted because that would be too bold. Besides, he wouldn't see her again, so it made no sense to act on this impulse. Even if the impulse was about to drive him out of his skin.

"Thanks. I really appreciate all you've done."

"Just doing my job," he said.

"Oh," she said, seemingly disappointed.

He wanted to take it back. He *was* doing his job, but that had changed quickly. The fact was, despite his fear of history repeating itself, he wanted to see Shanna again. He couldn't deny the strong connection between them, and he wanted to see where that would lead.

"I better get on the road. I need to get home so I can . . . you know . . . uh . . . look over my presentation . . . and . . . well, again, thank you."

She turned and started to walk away. Each step she took away from him made his heart ache. "Shanna?" he said.

"Yes?" she turned.

In a few steps he was to her. "I wanted to tell you something."

"Okay."

SHANNA STOOD THERE, her heart thumping, while she waited for Cole to tell her something. He was close enough to her that she could smell the faint scent of his cologne.

"It's just that . . . well . . ." he said, letting his sentence dangle.

"Go on." She hoped he was going to say something about seeing her again because she wanted to spend more time with him. She didn't know him well, but what she knew, she liked. And if the chemical attraction were any indication, this might be the beginning of something more amazing than she'd ever experienced.

He cast his gaze to the ground. "I wanted to tell you to have a safe trip."

"Oh." That was it? Surely, he could feel the connection between them. "Thanks. As long as my car doesn't break down again." She let out a strangled laugh. More than anything she wanted to feel his lips on hers. She focused on controlling her erratic breathing and settling her heartbeat so she wouldn't pass out right there. She turned toward her car and took a few steps when she felt his hand on her shoulder.

He whirled her around to face him, then pulled her close. A rush of electricity zipped through her. He peered at her and then slipped his glance to her mouth. He was going to kiss her. And she was going to relish every moment.

Tentatively his lips found hers and she could almost hear the crackle of energy between them. He tenderly caressed her jawline with his thumbs, and she melted into his embrace as his kiss became more confident. She'd never felt like this with anyone, not even Greg. Her whole self was hyper-aware—from the crown of her head to the tips of her toes—while their lips mingled together rhythmically, and currents of electricity rushed up and down her spine. Her heart beat so fast that she worried she might have a heart attack, but she was willing to take the risk.

When Cole finally pulled away, Shanna felt dizzy and breathless. That was a kiss she'd not soon forget—make that *never* forget.

"I didn't want you to leave without . . ." Cole didn't need to finish his sentence because Shanna understood exactly what he meant.

Sucking in a breath to steady herself, Shanna said, "What does this mean?"

"I think it means we want to see each other again." Cole laughed softly.

"But how?" Shanna didn't want to ruin the moment, but kissing Cole changed everything.

"I don't know. I only know I feel this . . ." He searched her eyes.

"Me too," she said, knowing, again, *exactly* what he meant.

"I know there's a lot working against us, but I think I've figured out a solution," he said resting his forehead against hers.

"You have?" Shanna smiled to think he'd been thinking about *her*, about *them*.

"We can make it work."

"We can?" Her legs felt like overcooked pasta.

"If we both want to," he said, pulling away and looking at her.

"I want to." She didn't know much, but she knew this.

"You do?"

"Yes," she said it with as much emphasis as possible.

"So, we both agree to explore whatever *this* is?" he asked.

She nodded so vigorously that she hoped she wouldn't give herself a neck injury.

"I can drive to Denver regularly. I can keep my apartment in Fort Collins." He moved a tendril of hair from her face, then let his finger follow her neckline, which made her skin erupt in goosebumps.

"And I can drive to Juniper Springs. Maybe I can make the River Room my regular?" she said.

He smiled. "I think we can arrange that."

Without warning, a ribbon of doubt sliced through her, making her shiver. "I'm just . . ." She cast her gaze away from him.

"What?" He cupped her chin in his hand and tugged it up so she'd look at him.

She wanted to be truthful. "A little hesitant."

"Because of what happened with Greg?" he asked.

"I don't have a great track record with long-distance relationships." Fear bubbled up and threatened to spill over.

He placed his hands on either side of her head, then peered deeply into her eyes and said, "Maybe the issue wasn't the long distance."

She looked at him.

"Maybe Greg didn't realize what an amazing woman you are and didn't make you a priority. Something I plan to do," he said with conviction. He moved his hands down and grabbed both of her hands in his.

"And you aren't scared?" she asked.

"Absolutely I am. You know I've been burned. Bad. But anything worth having is worth working for, right?" He squeezed her hands.

"Yeah."

"I don't know why I feel such a strong connection with you, but I want to see where this all goes. I want to take a chance," he said with fervor.

"Who knew my car breaking down would lead to this?" Falling for someone on the road to Amarillo was the last thing on her mind.

He laughed. "And when I got the call to tow your car, I never thought I'd find someone like you."

He leaned in and kissed her again. A kiss full of hope and meaning.

A kiss that told her that this was something different. A kiss that made her feel like she mattered to him. A kiss that held the promise of something spectacular ahead.

THE END

WANT to read more about Shanna and Cole? Be sure to check out *Journey to Juniper Springs* for the rest of their romance. Coming Fall 2022.

JOURNEY TO
Juniper Springs
JUNIPER SPRINGS
ROMANCE
REBECCA TALLEY

ABOUT THE AUTHOR

 Rebecca Talley grew up next to the ocean in Santa Barbara, California. She spent her youth at the beach collecting seashells and building sandcastles. She graduated from high school and left for college, where she met and married her sweetheart, Del.

Del and Rebecca are the sometimes frazzled, but always grateful, parents of ten wildly- creative and multi-talented children and the grandparents of the most adorable grandkids in the universe.

After spending nineteen years in rural Colorado with horses, cows, sheep, goats, rabbits, and donkeys, Rebecca and her family moved to a suburb of Houston, Texas, where she spends most of her time in the pool trying to avoid the heat and humidity. When she isn't in the pool, she loves to date her husband, play with her kids and grandkids, swim in the ocean, eat Dove dark chocolate, and dance to disco music while she cleans the house.

You can join her Reader News to keep up with her crazy life, including her new releases, and receive a free book, *Best Kind of Love,* at www.rebeccatalley.com

FREE Download

Will Brynn recognize the best kind of love when she sees it?

Best Kind of Love: A Reunion Romance Novella Kindle Edition

by Rebecca Talley ▾ (Author)

☆☆☆☆☆ ▾   98 customer reviews

amazonkindle

"This was a fantastic story!"
Gina K.

"The chemistry between the characters is great..."
Karen G.

When you join
Rebecca Talley's Reader News
you'll receive a complimentary copy
in your preferred format.

https://rebeccatalley.com/free-book-best-kind-of-love

187

BOOKS BY REBECCA TALLEY

Imperfect Love

Speak to My Heart

Grounded for Love

On Deck for Love

Flipping for Love

Wedding Weekend

Adding Christmas

PLEASE CONSIDER LEAVING A REVIEW

Reviews help authors find new readers and help readers find new authors. It's easy to leave a review on the book description page. Thank you so much!!